WHO WANTS THE DILETTANTE TO DIE?

GRACE PENNDRAGON

His dead brother's widow, a crazy cross between
bag lady and aristocrat?

SUSAN VANDERVOORT

His beautiful, illegitimate daughter, who resents
his sudden intrusion into her life?

BUNNY PENNDRAGON

His nephew and heir, unless Winslow succeeds in
changing his will?

DOLLY MORRIS

The pretty young housemaid who answered perfectly to the description of the type he can't resist?

LESLIE HOBBS

His bastard son, whose eagerness to inherit the old
man's fortune knows no bounds?

A DEATH FOR
A DILETTANTE

E. X. Giroux

BALLANTINE BOOKS • NEW YORK

Library of Congress Catalog Card Number: 86-26252

ISBN 0-345-34758-7

This edition published by arrangement with St. Martin's Press, Inc.

Manufactured in the United States of America

First Ballantine Books Edition: January 1988

*This book is for Betty and Harold Windover
and for days of* auld lang syne

PROLOGUE

Winslow Maxwell Penndragon was a dilettante in the true sense of the word. One of his nicer traits, and he had a number, was his acceptance of his life-style. No pretense was ever made that he cared for work or had any intention whatsoever of engaging in anything so demeaning. Luckily his father and his grandfather had labored industriously enough that their heir could do as he chose. What Winslow Penndragon chose to do was to gratify his every whim. Upon inheriting the Penndragon estate, he immediately liquidated the various business concerns so carefully nurtured by his sires, profitably invested the proceeds, and turned his attention to a varied and colorful life.

As was shortly apparent, Penndragon didn't confuse idleness with indolence. Many of his fads and pursuits were more exhausting and, at times, hazardous, than daily toil ever could have been. He roamed the world, finding and delighting in exotic places and dangerous situations. If his courage was ever in doubt, those doubts were laid to rest when Britain entered the lists against Germany in 1939. Penndragon had missed the First World War, but he wasn't about to miss this one. He returned to his country, took a commission in the Royal Air Force, and threw himself with enthusiasm and valor into the Battle of Britain. His was a charmed life. He was shot down over Germany, interned in a POW camp, promptly engineered a brilliant escape, made his way back to England, and became a legend in his own time.

Because of his rather girlish beauty, his meticulous grooming, and a penchant for outlandish vests, Penndragon was often suspected of being effeminate, perhaps homosexual. Actually he was robustly and lustily male. He was introduced to sex at the tender age of eleven by his mother's parlor maid. She was barely five years his senior, short and plump, apple-cheeked and dark of hair, and delightfully experienced. For the remainder of his life, Penndragon showed a decided preference for deliciously plump, dark-haired girls of the working class.

The years rolled by, wonderful years, thoroughly enjoyed by the dilettante. In his early sixties, he became interested in writing and turned out a number of adventure novels— lightly fictionalized with each hero bearing a striking resemblance to the author—that were fairly well received but certainly not best-sellers. World-wide fame arrived when he decided to spurn fiction and write a factual book with the unwieldy title of *How to Enjoy the Art of Dilettantism*. Recounting his own life proved to be juicy, exciting, violent, and, at times, outrageously funny. Penndragon was plunged into a new role, that of successful author, and took to it with his usual aplomb. He lectured to learned societies, gave informal talks, signed autographs, appeared on panel shows, and proved as gifted with the spoken word as the written one. He promptly wrote a second best-seller, this one called *The Diligent Dilettante*.

By the time Winslow Penndragon reached a hale and hearty seventy-one, his life was as rich and enjoyable as it had ever been. His health was excellent; he delighted in fine food; and his physical beauty survived the years; and in every way he was a happy, fulfilled man.

Then, without warning, the first ominous cloud appeared in the sunny heavens of Penndragon's private world. Astounded and completely nonplussed, he still had recourse to his favorite maxim—"Only the best will serve." With this in mind, he sought counsel from his godson, Chief Inspector Adam Kepesake of New Scotland Yard.

CHAPTER 1

Whether Chief Inspector Kepesake was the best is debatable. He was one of the better-looking inspectors, certainly the best-dressed, and he was fortunate in having the most-able detective sergeant at the Yard. Sergeant Brummell, christened Charles but known to all as Beau, was hard working, intuitive, and, for reasons many found mystifying, devoted to his superior officer. In appearance he was Kepesake's direct opposite. Brummell had the ability to make a new suit of clothes look like something picked up at a rummage sale; a freshly shaved face look as though it had rarely seen a razor; and a thick head of hair defy any comb ever manufactured. He also had tenacity, and that was evident as he slid a sheaf of forms into the in-basket on Kepesake's handsome desk.

"The superintendent says he has to have these today, Chief."

"Put him off. Tell him I'm up to my ears."

"I tried but he said—"

"I can guess what he said." Scowling, Kepesake inserted a fresh cigarette in his jade holder. "Chap's a ruddy slave driver. Well, let's get at it." He glanced up. "What is it, Helm?"

"A visitor, sir," the young constable told him.

"Make an appointment or have someone else handle it."

"Says it has to be you, sir. Sent his card in."

The chief inspector looked at the card and beamed. "Why didn't you say so? Bring him right in."

To Brummell's surprise, Kepesake, who rarely stirred from his office chair, sprang up and rushed to meet his visitor. Wonder whether he's a relative, Brummell thought, watching the men embrace. Sure dresses like the chief. Not that vest though! Even the chief wouldn't go that far.

Waiting until Kepesake had the other man ensconced in the most comfortable chair his office offered, Brummell asked, "Want I should leave?"

"No. Beau, I'd like you to meet Uncle Winslow. My sergeant, Uncle. Beau, you've heard of Winslow Penndragon."

"That I have. Recognized you right away, sir. Saw you the other night on television—that panel show. Liked how you managed to corner the psychologist."

Penndragon gave him the smile that was rapidly becoming famous. "It didn't take much effort. The man is a buffoon."

The sergeant swung on his superior. "You never told me that Mr. Penndragon is your uncle."

"Only a courtesy term, Beau."

"Adam is my godson," Penndragon explained. His glance flickered over Brummell's wrinkled suit, and he turned to Kepesake. "It's been . . . how long has it been since I've seen you?"

"Too long." Waving his holder, Kepesake peered through a cloud of smoke. "Nettie Kimshaw's garden party, last August. How's the family?"

"Bunny's fine. The amazing Grace is still as exasperating as ever. And your mother and father? In good health, I trust."

While Penndragon and Kepesake exchanged news, Brummell watched the older man with something approaching awe. To think he'd just shaken the hand of Winslow Penndragon. Wait until he told the wife about this.

Penndragon was as handsome in the flesh as on telly or in photos, with a mane of silver hair worn a bit long but suiting that face. Tall, slender, and well built, he had hardly a wrinkle and skin like a baby. Clothes—a beautifully tailored suit that had cost a mint, gray-silk tie the same shade as the suit, and a brocaded vest with swirls of lavender and rose and pale green against a silver-blue background. Have to have a lot of confidence to wear a vest like that. Fascinated, the sergeant watched as Penndragon extracted a cigar case and helped himself to a cheroot. Before the case was open, Kepesake was around the desk, flicking his lighter.

The two men had now worked through relatives and were catching up on tidbits about friends and acquaintances. Rather disconsolately, Brummell eyed the in-basket. Looked as though the superintendent was going to be raising hell about that stuff. Penndragon, who hadn't appeared to notice anything but his godson and his cheroot, followed Brummell's eyes. "Looks as though I caught you at a bad time, Adam."

Kepesake waved a dismissive hand. "It will wait. Must get one's priorities right. We'll have lunch at the club—"

"Sorry, this isn't a social visit."

"Do you mean you require our professional services?"

"Not the Yard's. Simply some advice."

Brummell started to rise. "Perhaps I'd better . . ."

"No." Penndragon waved him back. "You might be able to help."

"Tell us what we can do," Kepesake said earnestly.

For the first time since he'd entered the office, Penndragon seemed a trifle uncertain. "I have a spot of bother that needs looking into. A personal matter that demands discretion. I was wondering whether you could recommend a . . . I suppose a private inquiry agent is what I'm looking for."

"Oh." It was Kepesake's turn to look uncertain. "I imagine I can suggest several." He raised a brow at his sergeant. "What about Reynolds and that agency he started?"

"Depends on what Mr. Penndragon has in mind, Chief. Reynolds is reliable, but he's a bit of a rough diamond."

Grinding out his cheroot, Penndragon frowned. "A rough diamond is scarcely what I need. Specifically, the person I employ must be a gentleman or at least be able to act the part. This person will be required to enter my house and pose as a friend or acquaintance. He must be intelligent, capable, personable, and above all, discreet."

Kepesake smiled. "A tall order, Uncle Winslow. Most investigators are hardly the paragon that you're describing."

"I'm aware of that." Resting his snowy head against the chair back, Penndragon closed his eyes. Brummell had been unable to believe that this man was over seventy, but suddenly he looked his age. His delicate features were weary and incredibly fragile. He murmured, "Adam, I'm desperate. This is serious and could be . . . I think there is an urgency."

Kepesake lost his smile. He gazed at his godfather and then at his sergeant. "Any ideas, Beau?"

"One. But it's a long shot, Chief. We do know someone who fills the bill but—"

"For heaven's sake, Beau, spit it out!"

"The Farquson case. That business in Maddersley-on-Mead."

"Forsythe!" Penndragon's eyes snapped open and he sat up. "Robert Forsythe. Perfect!"

Kepesake raised his brows. "You know Forsythe?"

"We met once, but mainly I know him through newspaper accounts of his exploits. Amazing man."

"The reporters think so." Kepesake sighed. "As you know, he's a barrister and quite reluctant to being pulled into anything resembling detection. I doubt very much—"

"You've worked with him, Adam. Surely if you put a word in, he would consent to help me."

Brummell was shaking his shaggy head. "The chief's right, sir. Mr. Forsythe only helped us out because he had no choice. I don't think he'd budge on our say-so."

7

"But you can speak with him. At least ask him to see me. Once I talk to him I'm certain he can be persuaded."

"Of course I will," Kepesake assured. "I'll do all I can. I'll ring up immediately. When would you like to see him?"

"As soon as I can, if possible this afternoon." Penndragon reached for his cigar case. "This woman whose name is always linked with Forsythe. Just who is she?"

"Abigail Sanderson?" Kepesake busied himself lighting his godfather's cheroot. "Forsythe's secretary."

"I'm aware of that. But what is their relationship? Their names are always coupled."

Throwing back his head, Kepesake laughed. "If you're wondering whether it's romantic, I must disappoint you, Uncle. Miss Sanderson's not only old enough to be Forsythe's mother but she's acted like one ever since the death of his own mother. She was his father's secretary too and practically raised the boy."

"How old is she?"

"That's a secret." Brummell was laughing too. "Miss Sanderson is touchy about her age. Better keep that in mind. At a guess I'd say well into her fifties."

"And her employer?"

"Mid-thirties. Thought you'd met him."

"A number of years ago and at the time I barely noticed him." Penndragon stretched his slender frame. "Well, that's settled."

"Hardly," his godson told him. "You still have to persuade Forsythe."

"Adam, I have exceptional powers of persuasion." Penndragon flashed the famous smile. "Also, I have a habit of getting what I want. Devoted a lifetime to just that."

Brummell's first thought was that Penndragon was going to need all the persuasion at his command to sway Robert Forsythe. His second was that something was giving the man hell to make him so shaken and worried.

8

CHAPTER 2

RESISTING THE IMPULSE TO SLAM THE DOOR BEHIND HER, Miss Sanderson closed it softly and regarded the barrister with a blend of affection, anxiety, and exasperation. The affection was habitual. The anxiety and exasperation were emotions that had steadily been building since Forsythe's return from a disastrous fortnight in Switzerland. He slouched in the leather chair inherited from his father, one leg propped up on a hassock, his expression morose as he regarded the walking cast on that leg.

"What do you want?" he demanded.

"To straighten this room up. Mrs. Seton said you wouldn't let the cleaner in here this morning."

"Couldn't stand the woman fussing about. And that goes for you, too."

She calmly continued wielding the feather duster. "Sorry to interrupt your work, but this place looks like a pigsty." Circling behind his chair, she attacked the bookshelves.

"*What* work?"

"Good question. A bit slow, isn't it? Young Peters is winding up the Herald case and Vincent has the Montrose one well in hand. How are you feeling?"

"Nice of you to ask. I didn't think anyone gave a damn."

She paused and looked at the back of his long head. "Feeling sorry for ourselves, are we? Wallowing in self-pity?"

"Might as well. Obviously you haven't a shred of sympathy."

"I did warn you."

"I knew it! Now we get to the 'I told you so' lecture."

Taking a last flick at the books, she moved the duster along the wainscoting. When she didn't answer, he snapped, "Get on with it."

"I wouldn't stoop so low. Little late for it anyway. Anyone asinine enough to try to ski with a wonky knee like yours asks for a broken ankle."

"What was I supposed to do? Sit by the fire like an old man while everyone else was out on the slopes?" She shrugged and he bellowed, "Will you get out of here and leave me in peace!"

"As soon as I'm finished." Putting down the duster, she began emptying ashtrays. "Be a good boy and I'll bring you a mug of nice hot broth."

"I don't want broth. I want whiskey."

"Not with those painkillers you're gulping. Give them up or give up whiskey."

"Sandy, you're a hard woman."

She swung on him. "Look, I tried to persuade you to go down to the house in Sussex and relax until that ankle heals."

"And who would look after this practice?"

"The ones who are doing it now. Peters and Vincent and Mrs. Seton."

"But—"

"No buts. You're like a bear with a sore paw—completely unreasonable. If I pay attention to you, I'm fussing. If I don't, I'm a heartless fiend." She took a deep breath. "All you're doing by staying on in chambers is making us as miserable as *you* are."

He raised a hand. "You've made your point, Sandy, and

you're right. I was a fool to try to ski and I've been driving the staff mad. I suppose I should go down to Sussex, but Mrs. Meeks would drive *me* mad with her infernal coddling." He shifted his leg and winced. "I'm bored. Too much time on my hands and nothing on my mind."

She sank into one of the visitor's chairs. "I know it's irksome, and that knee must be hellishly painful too. Robby, you need a hobby."

"I have hobbies."

"Ah, but none you can manage at present." She ran a hand over her beautifully styled gray hair. "Why don't you go to Spanish classes with me?"

"I've no desire to speak Spanish. Besides, you've been toddling off to them for weeks and what have you learned?"

She cut loose with a torrent of Spanish and he grinned. "Sounds impressive, but what does it mean?"

"I asked, 'How much is it?' and then I said, 'That's too much.' I proceeded to tell you to do unspeakable things to either your mother or sister. My instructor tells me that such an expression would get one decapitated in a Spanish-speaking country. Then—"

"Sandy! What kind of teacher *is* this man?"

"Young and handsome and madly sexy, also amusing. You really should join Lino's class."

"I've no avid desire to be decapitated in Spain. Doesn't Lino teach you anything practical?"

"Certainly." She waved both arms and spat out more Spanish.

"The translation?"

"I just announced to all and sundry my desperate need for a bathroom. That practical enough?"

He nodded but was gazing past her shoulder with an abstracted expression. "I've been wondering whether what Sir Hilary said about me a number of years ago is the truth."

"And what is that?"

"We were involved with the Calvert case and Sir Hilary

11

told Melissa Calvert that I've a devious mind, more suited to detection than to law. I wonder whether he meant it."

"Only way to find out now would be to hold a séance. Sir Hilary, bless his rowdy soul, has been dead for years. What made you think of that? Tired of being a barrister?"

"Most of the time I wouldn't exchange law for anything else. But sometimes . . . right now . . ." He shifted his leg again. "Sandy, do you think crime detection could become addictive?"

She shook her head violently. "Not for me. Not after that grisly business in Maddersley-on-Mead." She eyed him with shrewd eyes. "Feel like you need a fix? Some nice juicy case with bodies bleeding all over the place?"

He avoided her eyes and she immediately started tapping her thumbnail against her front teeth. "Will you *stop* that?" he roared.

"Helps me think."

"That's the most infuriating habit. What are you thinking?"

"About coincidences. Mrs. Seton mentioned Adam Kepesake rang you up shortly before I came in and now you're raving on about detection being addictive. Methinks I smell a rat."

He stared at her. Such an austere face, he thought, such a deceptively austere face. Such a greyhound figure. Such an ability to look past his defenses with those cool blue eyes and expose any thoughts he had. He threw up his hands. "What's the use? No wonder I've never married."

"A number of times you've come close. What was the trouble? Afraid you'd never find a woman like me?"

"Afraid I would."

The cool eyes steadily regarded him. "Don't try to throw me off the scent. What did the rat want this time? Trying to drag you into solving another case for him?"

"This has nothing to do with the Yard. Kepesake merely wants me to speak to his godfather—"

"Who no doubt has any number of bodies bleeding all over *his* floor. Just who is Kepesake's godfather?"

"You'd never guess," Forsythe told her smugly.

"I'm not trying to."

"None other than the famous Winslow Maxwell Penndragon."

She jerked forward, a slow flush working up her thin face. "Blimey!"

"Thought that would shake you. Know anything about him?"

"After those books of his, I shouldn't think there are many who don't. Dilettante, wealthy, brilliant war record . . ." She grinned. "Sounds as though Penndragon practically held off the Luftwaffe singlehandedly. Been everywhere and done everything. I've a copy of his latest book in my desk—fabulously interesting. Must ask him to autograph it."

Forsythe smiled at her excitement. "I take it you aren't adverse to meeting this gentleman."

"I'm practically panting. But what does he want to speak with you about? Can't be legal expertise. Penndragon must have a battery of his own lads to keep up with the libel suits he has every time one of his candid books hits the market."

"I haven't a clue and neither did Adam Kepesake. But Kepesake did stress the necessity for discretion. I gather he dotes on his illustrious godfather."

"And so would I," Miss Sanderson said fervently. "What time may we expect him?"

Forsythe glanced at the ormolu clock on the mantelpiece. "If he's punctual, any moment now."

"Good Lord!" Her hands flew to her hair. "You could have told me sooner. I must look a fright."

"You look fine, Sandy. Calm down. I've seldom seen you acting so feminine."

"At least I managed to get this room tidied. Poor Mrs. Seton, she'll have a fit."

"Mrs. Seton wouldn't quiver an eyebrow if she ushered in the Prince of Wales. Ah, Mrs. Seton . . ."

For the first time since she'd joined the staff, Mrs. Seton

opened the barrister's door without knocking. Her normally stolid face was glowing. In a hushed voice she said, "Mr. Penndragon."

Forsythe started to push himself up and Penndragon told him genially, "No, stay where you are. Accident?"

"Skiing." He glanced past his visitor. Mrs. Seton was posted in the doorway, staring at Penndragon as though transfixed. "Thank you," Forsythe said and she backed out of the room, leaving the door ajar. She had to return to close it.

Penndragon shook his head. "Seems a nervous lady."

"Hardly. Your effect. Sandy, please bring up a chair. Mr. Penndragon, my secretary, Miss Sanderson."

The dilettante gave a courtly bow, gently pushed Miss Sanderson aside, and slid the chair up himself. Miss Sanderson, as transfixed as Mrs. Seton had been, fumbled for her own chair. Penndragon gallantly seated her before sinking into his. "We've met before," he told the younger man. "You may not remember . . ."

"At a dinner party given by . . . I forget the name, but it was around Christmas—about four years ago. I remember you well. You were recounting a trip to Tibet."

"You've a remarkable memory." Penndragon regarded the leg encased in the cast. "I had thought to ask your advice and help with a personal matter, but Adam didn't tell me you're immobilized."

"I doubt he's heard about my accident. I haven't seen him for months. As for being immobilized—" Forsythe waved an airy hand. "No difficulty in moving around. Simply a small bone broken."

His secretary wrenched her eyes from their visitor and glowered at Forsythe. After days of rushing around cosseting him—blimey, what a phony!

"Well, that *is* a relief. I'm counting on you and when I saw you I thought, well, that's out." Penndragon smiled at the barrister and let the tail end of that smile drift over his secretary. Miss Sanderson promptly beamed back. "I hardly

14

know where to begin. I suppose I must be blunt, but this is going to sound dreadfully dramatic. In the last week my life has been . . . Mr. Forsythe, two attempts have been made to kill me."

Miss Sanderson made a muffled sound and Forsythe raised his brows. "In London?"

"At my family home in Warwickshire. When I'm not traveling, I spend most of my time there. I maintain a pied-à-terre in the city, but I rarely use it. And that is the reason why this investigation must be discreet. I'm forced to face the fact that a member of my family or one of my servants is responsible." Penndragon shook a baffled head. "I simply can't believe that."

"You'd better give us the details," the barrister told him.

"The first attempt involved my car. It's a vintage Bentley, a car I'm extremely fond of. Five days ago I was going to drive to Coventry on a business matter. I'm a wretched driver and generally my nephew handles that chore, but that day he had a backlog of work—Bunny acts as my secretary—and I decided to drive myself."

"Were the members of your household aware of this?"

"Yes. I had mentioned it the previous evening at dinner." Penndragon glanced down at his hands. They were long, slender, graceful, and at that moment were twisting together in his lap. He reached for his cigar case, courteously raised an inquiring brow at Miss Sanderson, and when she nodded, lit a cheroot. "The Bentley had been in for servicing and my man Evans went into the garage early that morning to pick it up. While I was breakfasting, he brought it back and parked it in front of the main door. Evans assures me that the car was operating perfectly at the time. As soon as I had finished my breakfast, I paused in the hall for my overcoat and briefcase and then went directly to the Bentley."

With his eyes fixed on the glowing end of his cheroot, Penndragon said softly, "I find this most painful. Would you be kind enough . . . may I have a drink?"

Miss Sanderson poured a generous whiskey and soda for their guest, another for herself, and, ignoring Forsythe's imploring gesture, handed him a glass of soda. Penndragon took a long swig and continued, "The driveway is rather twisting, but nearer the road it straightens out into a steep slope. I've been told by my nephew that I have a habit of 'riding the brakes.' As I neared the gates, I braked sharply and discovered they didn't respond. Luckily I didn't panic. I steered the car, at quite a speed, between the gateposts and across the road, crashing into the embankment."

"Were you hurt?" Miss Sanderson asked in a hushed voice.

This time the smile was all for her. Penndragon stretched his long body and touched an arm and one hip. "Shaken and badly bruised but—" The smile vanished and his lips set. "The Bentley was badly damaged. The horrifying part is that if I hadn't braked at that time, I probably would have been killed. From my property the land falls in a steep and treacherous hill into the village, and there's no way I could have avoided a bad accident. In fact, if there had been another vehicle traveling along the road at that moment . . . well, I wouldn't be here telling you all this."

"You had the brakes checked," Forsythe said, and it wasn't a question.

"Of course. A capable mechanic has serviced my cars for years. He told me that after the Bentley left his garage that morning the brake connection must have been loosened. He found a spot where the car had been parked on the driveway that was drenched with brake fluid. I have sworn him to secrecy." Penndragon held up his hand. "I know what your next question is. It would have been fast and simple to do this. And the only time it could have been done was while I was breakfasting."

"Evans had an excellent chance to do it," Miss Sanderson said.

"Impossible! Evans and his sister have been in my employ for over twenty years." Penndragon gave a shaky laugh and held out his glass. Miss Sanderson refilled it, then her own, and took the one Forsythe was hopefully extending and splashed soda in it. Giving it a disgusted look, he pushed it away. Penndragon shook his head ruefully. "You're probably wondering whether I drink this much habitually. I don't. I suppose it's the strain. I have to consider that a member of my household wants me dead. Quite frankly, I can't believe it."

"Sadly enough the majority of murders are committed by a member of the family," the barrister told him. "Now, the second attempt."

"It happened two days after I smashed up the Bentley. I was still stiff and sore, but it was the one day a week that I work on the gardens. For early spring it was a fine day and I wanted to get some pruning done. I put on my gardening clothes and stopped at the tennis court on my way to the shed where I keep the rest of my gear—gloves, gardening hat, and so forth. A spirited game of singles was in progress, and I sat down on a bench to watch. Evans and my sister-in-law had come out of the house to watch and we cheered the players on.

"When the set was finished I went to the shed, put my hand on the knob, and was about to open the door when a guest, Susan Vandervoort, called to me. As I stepped back, I must have shoved the door. Something came plummeting down and there was a loud thud. Susan ran up and . . ." Penndragon paused and took a sip of his drink. "A piece of statuary that once had been part of a fountain had been stored on the floor at the rear of the shed. It had been chipped and I planned to have it restored but hadn't gotten around to it. A charming little piece of a small girl holding a seashell. Someone had balanced the statue on a narrow ledge above the door so that when the door was opened it would fall on whomever was underneath. I hardly need to tell you what the result would have been."

Miss Sanderson frowned. "Surely the person who put it up there would have been trapped in the shed."

"The shed has a sizable window at the rear. That window was open."

Templing his fingers, Forsythe regarded them. "So . . . nip in and lift the statue into place. Clamber through the window and away. Again fast and simple." He glanced up. "Why did your guest call to you?"

"Susan had just discovered a clump of daffodils that was in full bloom in a sheltered spot and wanted me to have a look. Unusual in March. Susan and the daffodils saved my life. Odd. Friends have always insisted that I have a cat's nine lives and I think I've believed it. I went through the war unscathed and I've been in positions where I *should* have died, and yet I lived through them. Certainly I've had mishaps—a fall and a broken leg in the Austrian Alps." He waved a negligent hand at Forsythe's cast. "A dislocated shoulder in Tunis and . . . all minor mishaps. I fear I've always taken life for granted. Fortunately I've a strong constitution and my physician tells me I'm in marvelous shape. I *enjoy* life and am looking forward to about another thirty—"

"Thirty," Miss Sanderson blurted.

Again she was bathed in his wonderful smile. She was practically purring as he told her, "Yes, thirty. I come from a long-lived line. When my grandfather died he was over a hundred and my father was eighty and in excellent health when he was killed in an accident. If that hadn't happened I imagine Father would have exceeded the hundred mark. Yes, Miss Sanderson, at seventy-one I'm looking forward to many more years. And no one is taking them away from *me.*"

"In that case we'd better narrow down the lists of suspects." Forsythe pushed his glass toward his secretary. "Sandy, I took my last medication almost four hours ago. Fill that up and I don't mean with soda."

This time Miss Sanderson knew better than to argue.

CHAPTER 3

WINSLOW PENNDRAGON WAITED UNTIL FORSYTHE HAD his drink and then he said slowly, "From here on it might be best if you questioned."

"My first question concerns the time element. You've pinpointed the time available to loosen the brake connection in the first attempt. Have you any idea about the second?"

"I can give you the precise amount of time. My gardener Jarvis was able to confirm that. It appears he entered the shed to get some tools shortly before I tried. At that point, the statue was in its usual place."

"And this was?"

"About half an hour before. From the shed you can see the tennis court, and Jarvis noticed me coming out the rear door of the house and pausing by the court. Then, of course, I became interested and sat down on the bench with my sister-in-law and Evans. As soon as the set was over, I went directly to the shed. So the statue had to have been lifted into place while I was sitting there."

"And again, the members of the household were aware you were gardening that morning?"

"Yes."

"Hmm." Forsythe stroked his chin. "This should make

it simpler. All we seem to have to do is eliminate the people who were with you during breakfast and the ones at the tennis court."

Penndragon shook his head. "That's where this whole affair becomes bizarre. In the breakfast room with me were two young guests—"

"I think," the barrister interrupted, "we'd better have the number of people in the house and their names."

"My staff consists of six including the gardener. There are two maids, but they're very young and have only been with us for a few months. Their names are Dolly and Geneva Morris and they're nieces of Evans and his sister Linda. The cook . . . Mrs. Krugger is out of the question."

"You mentioned Evans and his sister have been with you over twenty years."

"Close to twenty-one now. When they came to me, Evans was in his late twenties and Linda is much younger than he."

"How much?"

"At that time she was only sixteen. A lovely girl. Unfortunately her plumpness has disappeared under rolls of fat. Too bad. Little Dolly looks much the same now as her aunt did at the same age. Geneva is quite plain."

Flipping open her notebook, Miss Sanderson wrote down Evans and Linda Evans. On the other side of the page she put down Dolly and Geneva Morris, Mrs. Krugger, and Jarvis. "Then there is Grace Penndragon," Penndragon said, "the widow of my only brother. Gerald was much younger than I, but Grace is about my age. Gerald piloted a fighter plane too and was killed in 1945. His son was born after his death—about four months if I remember correctly—and I took the boy and his mother in. Gerald's son was named after me; it was his father's wish and Grace honored it, but he's always been called Bunny. Silly name, but somehow it suits him. I raised Bunny as my son and saw to his education. After he came down from Oxford, he decided

20

to remain with me as companion and secretary. It was his decision. I certainly didn't pressure, but I was delighted to have him with me. Bunny's extremely competent, wonderful at details about visas and traveling arrangements and so on."

Miss Sanderson added Grace and Winslow Maxwell II to her list. After the man's name she jotted down Bunny. She waited for the other names and when Penndragon didn't speak, she glanced up. Again his hands were twisting together in his lap. She lifted a brow at the barrister and he prompted. "Your guests?"

"Susan Vandervoort, Jason Cooper, and Leslie Hobbs."

"Are these people related to you?"

Penndragon crossed his long legs at the ankles, uncrossed them, smoothed down his flamboyant vest, and finally said, "Yes, but it's a bit complicated. May we leave this for later?"

"You said they were young," Forsythe persisted. "How young?"

"Young to me. Susan's thirty-one and Leslie and Jason a few months short of that age."

After she wrote the three names down, Miss Sanderson put a large question mark beside them. They waited and when Penndragon remained silent Forsythe said, "We'll return to the morning of the accident with the Bentley. You said two of your guests breakfasted with you."

"Susan and Leslie. Bunny finished his meal and left the room a few moments after I sat down. He had to put the necessary papers in my briefcase for my appointment in Coventry. Linda had cooked that morning as our cook was indisposed again—" Breaking off, he chuckled. "If Mrs. Krugger hadn't been enjoying ill health, I would have breakfasted in my own quarters. Mrs. Krugger is not only a confirmed hypochondriac but is the world's worst cook. Boils *everything*. Linda as well as being a fine housekeeper is also an adequate cook. She takes her meals with the family, so she'd arranged the food on hot plates and took her

21

breakfast with us. Evans was bringing the Bentley and Jason had gone out for an early walk. Grace was still in bed. She rarely stirs before ten."

Miss Sanderson looked up from her notebook. "So Susan Vandervoort, Leslie Hobbs, and Linda Evans couldn't have touched the car. Which leaves Jason Cooper, your sister-in-law, nephew, and Evans."

"Precisely."

The barrister eased his injured leg off the hassock, winced, and reached for his glass. As he drained it, he glanced at his secretary, appeared to reconsider a demand for more whiskey, and told the older man, "You said Evans and Mrs. Penndragon were with you at the tennis court. Who were the players?"

"My nephew and Jason Cooper. Now, do you understand how bizarre this is?"

Miss Sanderson glanced down at her notes. "The ones who could have fixed the brakes couldn't have touched the statue."

Springing up, Penndragon strode around the room. "I refuse to believe *two* people are trying to kill me! And what about motive? No member of my household has reason to want me dead. It has to be a maniac."

"Maybe two maniacs," Miss Sanderson muttered.

Forsythe followed the older man's movements. "It does seem farfetched, but the brakes were interfered with and that little statue didn't climb up over the door by itself. Let's begin with the most common motive—money. Who would gain financially by your death?"

"Bunny is my heir. There's a small income for life for Grace, several bequests to charitable institutions, a scholarship in my brother's name, and legacies for the servants. That's the way my will stands at present."

"Present?" Forsythe arched his brows. "You're considering changing the terms of your will?"

"Yes."

"Is your nephew aware of this?"

"He is. And of the reason for the change. But Bunny was right in sight while the statue was moved. Anyway, you'd have to know my nephew. He's not only incapable of violence but totally devoted to me."

"And Bunny couldn't have been working with his mother," Miss Sanderson pointed out. "Grace Penndragon was a spectator at the tennis game. Either of them could have drained the brake fluid, but neither could have made the second attempt." She frowned and added, "Linda Evans could have made the second attempt, but not the first. Her brother . . . vice versa. None of the guests could have done both."

"And none of these young people are mentioned in the current will." Forsythe said crisply, "I think you must tell us about your guests. You say they're all related to you?"

"Closely, the closest possible relationships." Penndragon stopped pacing and leaned against the back of his chair. "This is one reason why discretion is essential. Susan is my daughter; Leslie and Jason are my sons."

Miss Sanderson's mouth fell open. "But . . . I've read your books. You never married."

"Several times I considered it, but—" He flashed his warm smile. "Many people would accuse me of selfish motives in remaining a bachelor. And they're right. There's been no place in my life for a wife or children. But there was another reason, not quite as selfish. Until recently I've spent little time in England. I couldn't sentence a woman to a husband who rarely would have been with her or the children."

"What about your nephew and your brother's widow?" Miss Sanderson asked.

"Even when Bunny was in school, he spent his holidays wherever I happened to be at the time. As I mentioned, he's been my companion ever since he finished his education. As for the amazing Grace—"

"Why do you call her amazing?" Miss Sanderson asked.

"When you meet her, you'll see why. During the war

23

Grace had a most responsible job. She worked in the decoding department, quite hush-hush, and I understand she was one of their best cryptographers. Even now she's called to London when they have a knotty problem. Yet this woman, who's a wizard at codes, hardly knows what day it is. Spends most of her time working at word puzzles. As for neglecting Grace . . . well, frankly, we've never gotten along. I opposed her marriage to Gerald. Not only was she much older than my brother but completely unattractive—a scraggly looking woman without even the compensation of a nice personality."

"Yet she and her son did come to live with you," Forsythe remarked.

"Grace made clear that was only for Bunny's sake. My father left the bulk of his estate to me—Gerald was virtually penniless. I saw to my brother's needs during his lifetime and, of course, have looked after his family for forty years."

"Let's get back to your daughter and sons," Forsythe told him.

With a deep sigh, Penndragon sat down again. "I know this is necessary, but I'm finding it incredibly embarrassing. Very well. My three children are . . . my grandfather would have said they were born on the wrong side of the blanket. They're illegitimate. I can read your faces. You're thinking not only are they all roughly the same age but I must have been forty when they were conceived. I'll explain, but do keep in mind that I'm making no attempt to defend myself."

A slender hand stroked silvery hair away from his brow. "I'm a man of strong appetites. My sexual appetite operates with a specific type of woman. Another reason I've never married is that I'm drawn only to females I could never consider making my wife. These infatuations have always been brief. The only women I desire are very young ones, under twenty, and of similar physical characteristics—short plump girls with round faces and dark hair. And of the

24

working class—shopgirls, waitresses, domestic workers. There, I've bared my breast to you."

"In complete confidence," Forsythe assured.

This mention of confidence seemed to give Penndragon some.

"Over thirty years ago, to my complete shock, I found I had gotten three girls pregnant at the same time. Sally, Joyce, and Susan. Sally was a waitress in a café in Leeds; Joyce worked in a bookshop in a tiny village called Mousehole on the Channel; Susan in a women's clothing shop in London. I was candid with all three. From the beginning they knew I would never marry them, but as a man of honor that I certainly wouldn't desert them if they became pregnant. When I learned the situation, I immediately consulted with my solicitor—"

"Did these girls know about the others?" Forsythe interrupted.

"Of course not! They'd not the slightest suspicion they weren't the sole object of my interest. As I was saying, I consulted my solicitor and followed his advice. I settled an amount of money on each, had them sign statements agreeing they had no further claim on me, and told them they could take any course they wished. It was their decision whether they terminated their pregnancies or not. All three decided to have their babies."

Miss Sanderson was regarding him as though he'd just arrived from another planet. Forsythe looked at her uneasily. His secretary had a notoriously sharp tongue. But she simply asked, "Were there difficulties in persuading them to sign the statements?"

"Not really. Although they looked very much alike, they possessed very different natures. Sally—she was Leslie's mother—was a survivor, a pretty little piece but hard as nails. All she objected to was the amount of the cash settlement. Claimed it should have been more and had the temerity to threaten me with a paternity suit. I told her to sue and be damned, and quite sensibly she raised no further objections.

"Jason's mother—Joyce—was somewhat different, just as calculating but much more clever than Sally in concealing it. To my surprise, Joyce flared up and told me her only interest in me had been my money. I'd always thought she loved me. Not only was she insulting but she enjoyed every minute of it. Told me she hated men and would be most happy to raise her child by herself. She signed the statement, took the money, and booted me out."

Even after thirty years the memory still rankled. Penndragon was flushed and indignant. Hiding a grin, Forsythe said, "And the third girl, that would be Susan Vandervoort's mother."

"At the time she was Susan Miller. Susan was the youngest of the girls, barely sixteen and gentle, modest, and affectionate. Susan had shown no interest in expensive gifts; all she wanted was me. My interview with her was a painful ordeal for both of us. She made no mention of marriage, but she begged me to let her have some small corner in my life. Finally I convinced her it was over. She wept and clung to me and refused to take money. For the sake of her unborn child, I convinced her she must accept the settlement. She meekly signed the statement and we said goodbye. Of the three girls, only Susan loved me. After this was accomplished, I put them from my mind."

"But not their children," Miss Sanderson said hopefully.

"I could lie and give you the answer you'd like to hear, but the truth is that I forgot the children completely—until last October. As one grows older, there is a tendency to look backward in time. I'd never done this before, but on my birthday—I was on a lecture tour in New York—I suddenly realized I was seventy-one and my only relatives were a nephew and a sister-in-law whom I detest. I began to hunger for someone closer and regretted that I'd never married.

"My life has been devoted to my own gratification and I've always gotten exactly what I wanted. While I was feeling sorry for myself, I realized that I *could* have what I wanted. Somewhere I did have a family; somewhere I had three children."

26

"A case of having your cake and eating it too," Miss Sanderson muttered.

He lifted an ironic brow. "Exactly. Once I make a decision, I move rapidly. Before I returned to England, I had engaged a private agency to quietly undertake the task of finding my children and compiling histories of their lives. When I returned to England in mid-December, the information was on my desk. Before Christmas I had looked up all three and spoken with them."

His secretary seemed speechless and Forsythe asked, "Were you planning on adopting them?"

"No. My plan was this. I would meet them, persuade them to visit in my home for a month, and select one of them. I knew there might be some resentment toward me, but I hoped one might prove compatible and with that one I would share my life." Penndragon gave the barrister a shrewd look. "As the reports showed that my daughter and both my sons were in financial trouble, I sweetened the pot by offering each of them five thousand pounds for that month. I also hinted to all three that if we hit it off, he or she might be my heir."

"Blimey," Miss Sanderson breathed. "Did you tell them three people were competing?"

"Definitely not."

Forsythe tapped a finger against the edge of his desk. "You met them before Christmas. Did they immediately come to your home?"

"They arrived the first and second day of this month. I'd hoped to have them gathered in January, but . . . I think it best to explain just what happened when I met each of them."

Glancing at the clock, Forsythe said, "Time for tea. Sandy, would you do the honors?"

As the door closed behind her, Penndragon gave Forsythe a conspiratorial wink. "I hope I haven't shocked your secretary."

"Never fear. Sandy's appearance is deceptive. She's virtually shockproof."

27

"And the world condones this type of behavior now. Women boast about having children out of wedlock and no one seems to worry about marriage vows. Thirty years ago, society was much more narrow-minded and stern."

The men chatted about the changes in moral values until Miss Sanderson bustled in with a tray. With some amusement, Forsythe noted she'd outdone herself. She'd brought out the fine china and had managed to obtain dainty sandwiches and a profusion of small cakes. Penndragon's earlier reticence appeared to have vanished and between sips and bites he spoke freely.

"Leslie Hobbs was the first one I approached. He looks much like his mother, Sally—short, plump, and dark-haired. Sally turned out to be a shrewd businesswoman, but Leslie didn't inherit the trait. This was what had put him in trouble financially.

"Before his birth, Sally had used her settlement to buy the café where she worked and promptly married the cook, a man named Hobbs. The café proved to be a success, but her hasty marriage was a disaster. Hobbs was a heavy drinker and somewhat of a brute. He resented the baby and took every opportunity to punish him. Sally put up with it for six years, but then Hobbs beat the child badly, breaking Leslie's leg in two places, and when Sally tried to intervene, the man turned on her. She kicked Hobbs out and he died several years later.

"In time she set up other cafés in Leeds until she had a chain of five. From the time Leslie was old enough to act as a busboy, he was taught the business while his mother ran it. About two years ago, Sally was killed by a lorry while crossing a street and Leslie took control. Instead of carrying on with the cafés, he sold them out and came to London to open a rather pretentious restaurant. He decorated lavishly and hired a staff, including a Spanish maître d' and hostess, and a noted French chef. He overextended badly and also fell in love with his hostess Lola, who proved to be an expensive young lady. By the time I looked him up, he was terribly in debt. Not only is he in danger of losing the business but also Lola."

Miss Sanderson refilled the cups and nudged the cake plate closer to their guest. "What was your reception from Leslie Hobbs?"

"The second coming of Christ," he said dryly. "Sally had never made any secret about the boy's natural father. I got the impression both mother and son were proud of it, and I think both hoped I would re-enter their lives. To prove I was his parent, I took along the statement signed by his mother, but it wasn't necessary. Leslie was only too eager to go home with me at once, but I put him off. I did advance some funds to cover his more pressing debts. Then I sought out my daughter."

He selected a cake, put it on his plate, and looked dreamily past the barrister's shoulder. "Susan Miller had married too. She'd used her settlement to purchase a tiny dress shop, but she wasn't a good businesswoman. The shop didn't prosper and by the time her daughter was a toddler, Susan was in trouble. An admirer came to her rescue and put his savings into the business. Amos Vandervoort was much older than Susan; in fact, he's my senior by about ten years. They were married. Vandervoort adopted little Susan, and her mother and he eked out a living and raised the child. Apparently Vandervoort was devoted to both Susans. When my daughter was eighteen, Susan died and between Amos and young Susan, they managed to run the shop. Four years ago, he had a heart attack and then a stroke and Susan was forced to put him in a nursing home. She chose an expensive one and was unable to finance it from their tiny business income, so she sold it and took a position as a buyer with a large store. But even with a fair salary, she couldn't meet her stepfather's expenses. Susan is devoted to the man and, according to the report from the agency, lives frugally and cuts every corner to keep Vandervoort in his nursing home. But it isn't working."

"Your daughter must have been delighted when you went to her," Forsythe said.

"Delighted . . . no. I'd thought she would be anxious, perhaps depressed about her situation, but she seemed carefree and happy. She knew nothing about me and I had to show her the statement signed by her mother before she believed that I was her father. She didn't seem to resent it; in fact, she seemed . . . amused."

Miss Sanderson cocked her gray head. "Does Susan resemble her mother too?"

"Susan is a feminine version of me at the same age— similar bone structure and coloring. I was charmed. It was like looking into a mirror. I'd been disappointed in Leslie, but Susan . . . I pressed her to go home with me, but she simply laughed and said she would have to give it some thought. I hoped the cash offer would sway her, but she laughed at that too. Finally she said she would let me know her decision. I had to settle for that."

Her duties as hostess completed, Miss Sanderson leaned back and selected a cigarette; Penndragon hastened to extend his lighter. She blew a smoke ring, regarded it, and said, "Sounds as though you've made your choice."

Penndragon nodded. "I *was* impressed by my daughter. Her flat was tiny, but she'd made a bright and attractive home. Her mother's and stepfather's wedding picture was on the mantel with a bowl of small roses beside it. When I was there, she was decorating her Christmas tree and told me it had a theme. Her mother had collected little dolls in national dress from many countries, and Susan was hanging them on the tree. Little girls and boys from all over the world. Christmas carols were playing and it was so homey. I hated to leave without some commitment from her, but I didn't dare press. From her flat, I went to look up Jason Cooper. I admit I was of two minds on seeing the boy."

"Why?" Miss Sanderson asked.

"First, let me tell you Jason's history. Sally and Susan had both stuck with what they knew best—cafés and dress

30

shops. Joyce did too. With her settlement, she bought the bookshop in Mousehole, but she never married. She raised her son by herself. In Joyce's world, there was room only for Jason and I think she must have devoured the boy. No chance of a normal life for Jason or even another relationship. Toward the end, Joyce developed leukemia and was bedridden. She urged the boy to sell the shop in Mousehole and relocate in London. Still trying to run his life, of course. As usual, Jason obeyed and for the first time in his life he was parted from his mother. He came to London, spent six weeks locating a flat and a suitable location for his bookshop, and was called back to Mousehole about three weeks before I met him. I thought Joyce might . . . she might maliciously interfere with my plans for Jason.

"It took courage to enter her hospital room and face her. I didn't recognize her. She was so wasted and incredibly small. But her mind was still clear and much to my surprise, she seemed glad to see me. Jason was at her bedside and she introduced us in such a way that there was little awkwardness. Then she asked to speak privately with me, and Jason left us. Joyce said that even though she had renounced all legal claim on me, I must help our son. She told me their troubles, but I already knew that the new shop would be financially difficult to handle. I assured her that if Jason would visit me for a month, I would see that he had ample funds to get started, and she promised she would see that he did. But, as I soon found out, she hadn't really softened. She proceeded to tell me exactly what she thought of me. She still hated me and called me callous, selfish, a satyr. She ordered me to do the right thing by her boy or she would come back and haunt me." Penndragon laughed. "If anyone is capable of that, Joyce was."

"She must have kept her promise," Miss Sanderson said.

"She did. A few days later she died and after her funeral, Jason rang me up and told me he was at my disposal. His mother had extracted a deathbed promise from the boy."

The secretary made no effort to hide her curiosity. "What is Jason Cooper like?"

"In appearance, he's a combination of Joyce and me. He has my height and build and his mother's coloring—brown eyes and hair and olive skin. Jason has been living in my home for almost two weeks and I still know nothing about him. Joyce was a dominant woman and perhaps the boy simply never developed a strong personality. He's . . . I suppose the word is inscrutable—like a wooden Indian."

Tapping a thumbnail against her front teeth, Miss Sanderson pondered. It was Forsythe who said, "Both Leslie and Jason were willing to come whenever you asked. What was the delay?"

"Who rather than what. Susan was the delay. At Christmas, I selected some porcelain figures of children for her tree and had them delivered. I thought she'd be in touch to thank me and agree to my request, but I heard nothing from her. In early January, I became impatient and rang up her flat. The caretaker told me that she'd moved suddenly, just before the new year, and had left no forwarding address. Then I rang up the store where she worked and was told she'd taken a leave of absence and hadn't left a number where she could be reached. I thought of getting in touch with her stepfather's nursing home, but decided against it. In the meantime"—Penndragon's lips twisted—"Leslie Hobbs was driving me frantic. He kept ringing up and asking when. I put him off.

"By the middle of February, I was rapidly losing patience and was about to resort to the private agency again when my daughter finally rang me up. Susan said her stepfather had suffered another stroke and that she'd taken a room close to the nursing home to be near him. But his condition had stabilized and she was willing, if I still wanted her, to come to Penndragon on the first day of March. I urged her to come immediately, but she said she hadn't been feeling well herself and we settled on the date she'd selected. When Evans brought her from the station, I was dismayed. She was thinner, washed-out, ill looking. Her high spirits had vanished and she was abstracted and depressed. She explained that the doctors thought Amos Vandervoort might die at any time."

"What were the reactions of your children when they met?" Forsythe asked.

"Not quite what I had expected. Leslie arrived the day before Jason and Susan. He drove up from London in an expensive sports car. The following morning, Jason arrived by the early train and that evening Susan by the late one. Leslie put on a great show of being overjoyed to learn that he had a brother and sister, but Susan and Jason seemed completely indifferent not only to Leslie but to each other. Of course, Jason is grieving for his mother and Susan is worried and anxious about her stepfather."

Miss Sanderson frowned. "I would have sworn there would have been fireworks—three people who never knew their father and were suddenly faced not only with that father but with brothers and a sister. How did the other members of your family react?"

"Much to my surprise, Grace, who seldom bothers with anyone, seemed to take a fancy to Susan. Bunny is pleasant to both my sons, but it's obvious he's smitten with my daughter."

"And your children's reactions to their aunt and cousin?"

"Again, Leslie acts overjoyed. Immediately started calling them Cousin Bunny and Aunt Grace. Susan and Jason?" Penndragon shrugged an elegant shoulder. "As far as they're concerned, Grace and Bunny could be pieces of furniture." He spread his hands. "And that, Mr. Forsythe, is about all I can tell you."

"Not quite. I've a hunch you can tell us the murderer's name."

Penndragon's eyes widened. "It would appear I've chosen wisely. You *are* a detective."

CHAPTER 4

Miss Sanderson sat tensely, her eyes wandering from the barrister's face to Winslow Penndragon's. Again, the older man's hands were twisting together, but that was the only sign of agitation. "Yes, Mr. Forsythe, I've thought this through and have been forced to conclude that the danger to me arrived with my three children. I believe Susan Vandervoort, Jason Cooper, or Leslie Hobbs has twice tried to kill me."

"They couldn't have," Miss Sanderson blurted. "You've proven that none of them could have made *both* attempts."

"One of them could have a confederate," Penndragon said gravely, "someone not connected with my home, a stranger who crept onto my grounds and ruined the brakes or put the statue above the shed door at the direction of one of my children."

Miss Sanderson's chin jutted. "That would be incredibly stupid! Any chance of inheriting or even a prospect of future financial help would be gone with you dead."

"Sandy," Forsythe said, "there are other reasons for murder besides gain."

"Revenge or hatred or fear," Penndragon said somberly. "Yet, I can't believe any of them feels those emotions for me."

"You did desert their mothers," Miss Sanderson pointed out.

"After providing for them. Sally, Susan, and Joyce possibly had better lives than they would have if they'd never known me. As for their children . . . all three had decent homes, ample funds, devoted mothers."

"Leslie's home wasn't so decent," Miss Sanderson reminded. "A drunken brute of a stepfather who broke his leg in two places."

"By the time Leslie was six, his stepfather was gone. Anyway, Hobbs was Sally's choice, not mine." Turning abruptly away from the secretary, Penndragon faced the barrister. "Do you agree with my reasoning?"

"Some of it. However, you did ask for advice. You have two courses. For your own safety you could leave your home, possibly leave England. Or—"

"I will not run," Penndragon snapped.

"—or get to the bottom of this."

"That I intend to do. Will you help me?"

Forsythe didn't hesitate. "Yes. But I must make it clear that I could fail. Twice your life has been in jeopardy. This is a determined and possibly clever person. I'm unable to give you my guarantee that I can prevent a third attempt."

"I ask for no guarantees. I make only one condition. When—I won't say if—you discover the identity of this person, your work is done. I won't tolerate interference from the police."

"But—"

"On this point I'm adamant. I'll deal with him or her myself."

"I'll not be a party to personal vengeance."

"There'll be no vengeance. That I promise. I'll simply clip a wing so that no further effort to harm me will ever be made."

"You won't take the law into your own hands or use violence?"

"You have my word."

35

"Very well. I'll do my best."

Penndragon made no effort to shake hands to seal the bargain. A complacent man, Miss Sanderson thought, never for a moment considering Robby might have refused to investigate. A man who'd always gotten what he wanted and fully expected to have the person responsible for two efforts to kill him delivered into his hands.

Forsythe cleared his throat. "Now for details. I'll have to come to your home, of course. How will you pass me off?"

"As a friend . . . no, that won't wash. Neither Grace nor Bunny would believe that. Hmm." Penndragon plucked at his lower lip. "I think your father was a member of one of my clubs."

"Which one?" Penndragon named the club and the barrister nodded. "Father was a member and so am I, although I rarely use it."

"Right, a club member, merely an acquaintance, having sticky problems with an injured ankle and in need of a rest in the country. And the clincher . . . have you ever done any writing, Mr. Forsythe? Come to think of it, we should be on a first-name basis from here on, Robert."

"Some," Forsythe said modestly. "I've been working on a treatise on criminal law begun by my father—"

"Intermittently," Miss Sanderson said scathingly, "and for years."

Penndragon paid no attention to the interruption. "That makes it even more plausible. Gives you the excuse to bring Miss Sanderson—"

"Abigail," the secretary said rather coyly.

"Abigail with you. As a fellow writer it's only natural I would extend the invitation to both of you."

"I was wondering whether you wanted me," Miss Sanderson said, and added smugly, "Winslow."

He turned to her employer. "I'll be driving home tomorrow and would be delighted to take you and your charming secretary with me."

Forsythe didn't look delighted. "You drove down?"

"Hardly, not after my last experience behind a wheel. I came by train, but I'm hiring a car and driver to return to Penndragon, so you needn't worry. The car won't have been interfered with and the driver is an expert. What time can you be ready?"

They settled on a time and then Penndragon rose, tugged his garish vest into place, and asked, "Any further questions?"

"One," Miss Sanderson said, "that description of your cook. Why on earth did you employ her and why keep her on? Has she been with you for years and you hate to discard her?"

"Mrs. Krugger is a rather recent addition. She came to us about . . . perhaps four years ago. My sister-in-law hired her. Apparently she hit it off with the woman and as Grace hardly knows what she's eating, she seems satisfied with the cook. I generally cook for myself in my own quarters. I feel sorry for Bunny and often have him in for a decent meal. And, as I mentioned, Mrs. Krugger has imaginary illnesses that frequently lay her low and Linda takes over."

"I still don't understand why you don't get rid of her. From your books, I assume you're something of a gourmet."

"I am and that's precisely why I put up with Mrs. Krugger. In one area, I've never met her equal. She serves the most appalling boiled messes and yet she's a superb baker—her bread, cakes, pastry . . . *heavenly.* Unfortunately, she's temperamental, only bakes when *she* wishes to. Once each year she makes a divine cake—brandy-swathed and filled with cherries. She refuses to serve it until it's reached the peak." He smiled at Miss Sanderson. "We're about due for one of them and you may have a chance to taste it. Then you'll understand why Mrs. Krugger remains in my house. Now, Robert, do you have any questions?"

"Yes. Sandy and I . . . we've received a certain amount of publicity. There must be many people who know

37

that we've been connected with other murder cases. After two attempts on your life, don't you think the members of your household will suspect why you're bringing us to Penndragon?"

This time Penndragon's smile was complacent. "If they knew about the attempts, yes."

"But they must know."

"I carefully concealed both from them. The car accident was easily explained away—simply my atrocious driving, which all of them accepted."

"But Miss Vandervoort was right there when the statue nearly fell on you."

"Susan is convinced that was an accident. I told her that I'd asked my gardener to move the statue to provide more floor space in the shed and that Jarvis had foolishly put it on the ledge."

"And she believed that?"

"Jarvis is quite old and doddering, and I pretended great indignation at his stupidity. Yes, Susan believed me. So, you needn't worry. Not one of them suspects a thing."

Miss Sanderson said crisply, "With the exception of the person or people who made the attempts."

"Of course."

After a moment, Forsythe nodded. "We've covered everything we can at this time."

"Until tomorrow, then." Penndragon moved toward the door and Miss Sanderson hurriedly rose to show him out. There was no necessity. Mrs. Seton, blushing furiously, was posted outside the door. Putting one possessive hand on his arm, she escorted him to the front door. Shutting the door, the secretary said hotly, "Robby, she had no business to do that! *La perra!*"

"Careful, Sandy. *That* I understood. Your Lino seems to specialize in curses."

Remorsefully, she gazed down at the tea tray. "I really shouldn't have called her a bitch."

"That's true. You've a nasty tongue at times and I was on pins and needles fearing you'd use it on Penndragon."

"Why on earth should I have?"

He grinned. "I've seen you cut people to shreds on less provocation than our professional dilettante gave you. Sit down and let's run over this business."

"It's late. Aggie will have dinner ready and then I'll catch it. What a dictator! I've the nerve to ask Winslow why he doesn't get rid of his cook and *mine* tells me when to get up, when to go to bed, and to be sure and eat my carrots."

"Aggie will have to wait. Blame it on me." His secretary shrugged and perched on the chair recently occupied by their illustrious guest. "Now, what do you think of our friend Penndragon?"

"Not a friend. We're simply useful in clearing up the trifling matter of who's trying to knock him off. What do I honestly think of him?" She said dreamily, *"Magnifico."*

"In basic English, Sandy."

"In basic English, the man is an unmitigated snob. Couldn't possibly marry a girl from 'the working class.' Also—what was it Joyce Cooper called him? A satyr. Sowed copious amounts of wild oats with mere children. He should be despicable, but he isn't. Somehow ordinary rules don't apply to him. I should loathe everything he stands for and yet . . ." She looked sheepishly at the barrister. "I find I'm yearning to be under twenty, chubby, and dark-haired, perhaps a barmaid. I must be getting senile."

He looked fondly at her. "Then so am I. He had somewhat the same effect on me. *Cojeanos del misso pie, compadre.*"

Her pale blue eyes widened. "That's Spanish. You never let on—"

"Only a few phrases, Sandy."

"What did you say?"

"We both have the same weakness, friend. As for the spell Penndragon casts, its content is probably twofold. One part is charisma—"

"He does ooze charm."

"The other is that he's a member of a rare species. Ever met a true dilettante before?"

"Never."

"I doubt we ever will again. The man is well worth keeping alive."

She was tapping her nail against a front tooth; Forsythe winced, but said nothing. Finally she said slowly, "That may not be possible. He's wearing blinders."

"And those blinders are made of sheer vanity. Penndragon refuses to believe that a servant in his employ might want him dead. He refuses to believe that a nephew threatened with disinheritance might kill him."

She bobbed her gray head. "Or that a sister-in-law who has reason to hate his guts might try to knock him off. But he was right about one thing. No one could have made both tries."

"He was right about another thing. There has to be a confederate, but not necessarily an outsider. There are any number of combinations."

"Agreed. One of the established household working with one of the prodigal children. Two of the children working together. Revenge, hatred, fear, gain . . . so many possible motives."

With an effort, Forsythe hoisted himself up and reached for his canes. "When we get to Penndragon, perhaps we can untangle them."

Miss Sanderson rose and their eyes met. "He should run for it."

"What was that famous quote from the war years? 'Never have so many owed so much to so few.' Sandy, Penndragon was one of the gallant few." As he hobbled toward the door, he said soberly, "He'll never run."

CHAPTER 5

Winslow Penndragon did things with flair. The hired car proved to be a limousine chauffeured by a strapping young man in a trim uniform. Brushing protests aside, Penndragon insisted on sitting in front to allow maximum room for his guests. Considering the circumstances, Forsythe was as comfortable as he could be. He stretched out on the wide cushioned seat, his injured leg supported on a jump seat. His secretary huddled in a corner, gazing sometimes through the window at the passing countryside and at other times through the thick pane of glass at the back of Penndragon's snowy head and tweed-clad shoulders. The tweeds were suitable for a country home, but with them he wore another startling vest, this one of daffodil-colored suede. The man certainly had a penchant for outlandish vests. She turned to share this thought with her companion, but Forsythe had closed his eyes and appeared to be dozing. She regarded him anxiously. Although he had made no complaint, she sensed he was in pain. As she watched him, his eyelids quivered and his eyes opened. "Must be nearly there, Sandy."

"Can't be much farther. How are you feeling?"

"Bearing up."

"When did you last take a pill?"

"Haven't had any today. When we get to Penndragon, I

plan to down several whiskeys. Seem to be more effective than those painkillers."

"Down too many and you'll probably fall and break your other leg." Miss Sanderson peered out of her window. "For your information we're going through a village and I see the beginning of what looks like that steep hill Winslow mentioned."

The limousine glided to the top of the hill and turned smoothly between the gateposts. For a time, the driveway rose steeply and then leveled out, zigzagging between low stone walls that balanced terra-cotta urns holding neatly trimmed shrubs. Beyond them stretched the gardens. "Nice layout," Miss Sanderson said. Then she blurted, "My God! Robby, sit up and take a look at the house."

He struggled up. "To put it mildly—eccentric."

Penndragon was a substantial and quite undistinguished manor house, but what riveted the eye was the edifice tacked to one side of it. A tower, built of yellowish rock and a great deal of glass, reared up over the slate roof of the main house. It might have looked at home as a castle keep, but here it looked unsightly and ridiculous. Their host had swung around and was smiling broadly at their expressions. He pushed aside the glass panel. "Shocking, isn't it?"

"Worse than that," Miss Sanderson said bluntly. "Wished on you by an ancestor who took leave of his senses?"

"My own doing and completely sane. I find Grace trying to live with, so when Bunny was a small chap, I had my own quarters built."

"But a *tower*?"

"I'd always wanted to live in a tower. Wait until you see the interior."

The car drew to a stop before the massive door of the manor house and Miss Sanderson scrambled out and stretched. Penndragon and the chauffeur assisted Forsythe. While their host proceeded to give directions about luggage, Miss Sanderson had a second shock. She nudged Forsythe. "What is *that*?"

That proved to be a scarecrow wandering along the driveway. As it drew closer, they could see it was an elderly woman wearing high rubber boots, a brown skirt with the hem dripping down, a matching jacket bereft of buttons and secured with countless safety pins, and a straw hat anchored under a sharp chin by a bright scarf. She carried a string shopping bag stuffed with newspapers, magazines, and a single Argyle sock.

"*Alice Through the Looking Glass,*" muttered Miss Sanderson. "A twin for the White Queen."

Forsythe chuckled. "Beau Brummell's female counterpart."

"A New York bag lady," Penndragon told them. "Otherwise known as the amazing Grace." He raised his voice. "Grace!"

The apparition paid no attention and seemed to be about to wander on. Taking two long strides, Penndragon tapped her shoulder and pointed at the highest safety pin. She nodded and fumbled inside the jacket. "Will you stop doing *that*!" he bellowed. He lowered his voice. "She turns off her hearing aid at the damndest times."

"Don't shout," his sister-in-law snapped. "I can hear you loud and clear."

"Our guests, Grace—"

"*Your* guests."

Penndragon shot an embarrassed glance at Forsythe and Miss Sanderson and proceeded to introduce them. Grace pushed horn-rimmed glasses up on her short nose and peered at the barrister. "Another writer, huh?" She turned her attention to his secretary. "You look like a useful person. Have something in common with Bunny. He fetches and carries for a writer too." She turned away and then, perhaps feeling she must make an additional effort, called, "*Try* to have a nice time." From her expression, it seemed she considered that impossible.

Her brother-in-law spread expressive hands. "I said you had to meet her."

Miss Sanderson watched Grace Penndragon disappear

43

around the corner of the house and then jerked to attention. Another person was approaching, this time from the opposite direction. A woman, but that was all she had in common with the scarecrow. She was a willowy young woman dressed modishly in tight pants, a gray silk Russian blouse, and one of those berets worn by painters to keep paint out of their hair slanting over an eye. The straight flaxen hair that cascaded over her shoulders was worth protecting. Her resemblance to their host was uncanny. Penndragon's dove gray eyes, fine features, and flawless skin were framed by those shimmering sheaves of hair. But her cheeks contained no trace of the peach bloom that colored her father's face. The girl was chalky.

"Susan," her father called, "please give our guests a warmer welcome than your aunt just did."

Their welcome from Susan Vandervoort, while certainly not warm, was polite. She asked all the correct questions and made all the correct responses, but her voice was flat and disinterested. Her father was regarding her with worried eyes. "It's cool, my dear; shouldn't you be wearing a jacket?"

"I'm quite warm enough, Winnie."

"Please don't call me that."

She lifted mocking eyes. "I thought we decided Mr. Penndragon was too formal."

"I asked you to call me Winslow."

"I prefer Winnie." She turned to the barrister. "I understand you're a writer like Winnie."

"Hardly. Certainly not in the same league as your father—"

"Winnie is not my father. *My* father is in a nursing home and very ill."

With this curt remark, Susan seemed to feel that she had discharged her social duties. She nodded at Forsythe and his secretary, turned away, and followed Grace's route around the house. Penndragon shook his head. "Sorry. You're not receiving much of a welcome. Grace is always impossible and Susan . . . she's a bit thorny."

44

"Not to worry," Forsythe reassured. "But I really should get off this leg."

"Again sorry. Come in and we'll get you settled." Penndragon led the way up the shallow steps and Forsythe, with the help of his canes, hobbled along behind. The entrance hall was spacious and had a soaring ceiling. Doors opened off of it, but Forsythe was gazing forlornly at the curving staircase. Taking his arm, Penndragon guided him to a bronze grill set into the far wall. "This will make it easier for you. A lift—installed by my father. Not for himself. Father delighted in racing up and down stairs, but Mother was rather frail and she used it."

As he reached for the grill, the door opened and a short woman bounced out. Definitely bounced, Miss Sanderson thought. She was shaped like a rubber ball with a round head balanced on plump shoulders. Her dark hair was close-cropped and the round face nestled on a series of chins. "Where is your brother?" Penndragon asked. "The driver needs help with the bags."

"In the pantry washing decanters."

"And why aren't you in your kitchen making dinner?"

A shoulder moved in a ponderous shrug. "It's no longer *my* kitchen. Mrs. Krugger is on her feet again and booted me out."

Penndragon groaned. "Just my luck. I'm dining with you tonight. The sacrifices one must make."

"Never mind, Mr. Penndragon," she consoled. "Mrs. Krugger is complaining of lower-back pain."

"Thank the dear Lord for that. Linda, I'd like you to meet our guests. Miss Sanderson and Mr. Forsythe. Robert, Abigail, Linda Evans."

The housekeeper offered them a plump hand and a warm smile. "I'll take you up to your rooms." She glanced at Forsythe's cast. "You'll have time to rest before dinner and, if you wish, I'll have it taken up to you."

"Robert will join us for dinner," her employer told her. "He must meet the rest of the menagerie."

"Menagerie? I take it he's already met Mrs. Penndragon."

45

"That he has." Penndragon turned to his guests. "You're in good hands. I'll see you at dinner or at least at what Mrs. Krugger considers dinner."

They were indeed in good hands with Linda Evans. The lift wafted them up to the next floor and she led the way along the hall, tossing bits of information over her shoulder. "Only a few steps. I made up Mr. Penndragon's father's suite for you." She opened a door. "Your room, Mr. Forsythe. Miss Sanderson, yours is through there. Bathroom between." She made a sweeping gesture. "This was a study and when we converted it to a bedroom, we decided to leave some bookshelves and many of the books. Bedroom area here, sitting area near the windows. There's a desk for you, Mr. Forsythe, and I had my brother move in a reclining chair so that you can pamper your leg a bit. If you need anything, ring. Geneva will look after it." She paused by the door. "Your luggage will be up directly."

As soon as she left, Forsythe headed to the recliner and eased his leg up. He glanced around approvingly. The room was huge and the sitting area furnished with chairs and side tables as well as a desk. A small bar was squeezed between bookshelves, and it looked well stocked. There were thoughtful touches—an excellent reading lamp at his elbow, a vase of pink carnations on the desk, a row of filled bowls on the bar.

As Miss Sanderson made her way back through the bathroom, she echoed his thoughts. "Penndragons live well, Robby. My room's as nice as this one. Doesn't have a bar, though. Care for a small libation?"

"I thought you'd never ask. Make that a large whiskey if the supplies run to it."

She investigated the row of decanters. "Anything your little heart desires, including a wee fridge with ice." Ignoring ice, she poured two whiskies.

Forsythe took a long drink and sighed with satisfaction. "What's in the bowls?"

She lifted the glass tops. "Salted nuts, crisps, dried fruit. From the sound of Mrs. Krugger's dinner, better have some."

The barrister munched nuts and finished his drink. "Any impressions?"

"This would be a dandy spot to vacation if our host wasn't a target for a killer." She bit noisily into a crisp. "The amazing Grace seems to be a dingbat and Susan Vandervoort looks like a ghost and obviously isn't trying to curry favor with her wealthy papa. Linda Evans . . . odd attitude for a servant. Shows familiarity with her boss and has a decidedly proprietary attitude toward this house. *'We decided'* and so on."

"Well, at least she's a jolly woman."

"Must have been a pretty girl. Her skin's nice and she has gorgeous eyes. Hmm." Miss Sanderson munched another crisp. "Sixteen and short and plump . . . I wonder."

"Don't jump to conclusions."

"What I'm going to jump into is the shower and some fresh clothes. Aren't you planning to change?"

"They'll have to make allowances for my invalidism."

She snorted. "That's not the way I heard it." She tried to imitate his voice. "No difficulty in moving around at all. *Boniga!*"

He grinned. "You certainly picked up some nasty Spanish words. When we meet the family around the dining table, try not to use any."

They met yet another family member before they reached the dining table. They were walking toward the lift when an Irish retriever came bounding up to them, stopped and sniffed at Forsythe's trousers, and proceeded to gnaw at one of his canes.

"Easy, boy!" Grasping the collar, Miss Sanderson hauled the animal back. She glanced at the man approaching them. "Lively dog."

"Behave yourself, Helter," the man commanded. "Yes, he's a bit rough, but he has an even temperament. Not like his mate here." He pointed down at the retriever at his heels. "Skelter's in a delicate condition and tends to be somewhat aggressive at the best of times. No, don't touch her. She nips."

47

Miss Sanderson hastily pulled back her hand. It was obvious from the sagging chestnut belly that Skelter was in quite a delicate condition. Showing a fine set of teeth, the bitch backed away from the strangers. Her owner extended a friendly hand. "Miss Sanderson and Mr. Forsythe, I'm Bunny Penndragon."

"Another useful person," Miss Sanderson told him and shook hands.

"Ah, you've met Mother." He grinned. "Has a fixation that all secretaries do is fetch and carry. We know better, don't we?"

Forsythe smiled at him. "I do anyway. Sandy is like another hand."

Bunny glanced down at the cast. "Looks as though you could use an extra hand now. I'll shoot you down in the lift and take the dogs down the stairs. Meet you in the hall and we'll get you off that leg."

When the grill slid back, Bunny was waiting. Both dogs were sprawled in front of double doors to the left. He waved a hand. "Uncle's domain. The mutts seem to feel called on to guard it, and Uncle Winslow can't stand dogs."

Bunny looks a little like a dog himself, Miss Sanderson decided. A nice dog with an equable disposition. He was as tall as his uncle, but with a heavier build. His hair was lightly dusted with gray and his eyes slanted down at the outside corners. Folds of skin below those eyes gave an appearance of sadness, but there was a twinkle in those brown doggy eyes and lines of humor around his lips. "On to the drawing room," he told them cheerfully. "We have a little drinking session before dinner. Always sherry. Some sort of tradition."

He ushered them into the drawing room, found comfortable chairs, and waved at his uncle who was presiding at the drink table. Penndragon poured sherry and gave the glasses and orders to his nephew. "Introduce our guests around. They've already met Susan and Linda."

Bunny took sherry and two young men over. "Jason Cooper and Leslie Hobbs," he announced and then wandered away toward Susan Vandervoort.

The taller man, Cooper, gave them a curt nod, but the shorter man was more expansive. Hobbs gave them wide smiles, warm and somewhat moist handclasps, and offered solicitous inquiries as to the condition of Forsythe's leg. Then they too wandered away. Jason returned to a chair near the hearth; Leslie posted himself near the drink table and his father. Penndragon paid no attention to his son. He was glancing around the room with an expression of vexation. "Bunny," he called. "Your mother isn't down. Has she turned off that blasted hearing aid again and didn't hear the dinner bell?"

"I'll check," Bunny said and started toward the door. "Ah, here she is now."

"Indeed I am," Grace Penndragon said. "As for turning off that blasted hearing aid, I feel no need to. As you'll notice, Winslow, I'm also wearing my glasses." She accepted a glass from her son and steered a course toward the new arrivals. "My brother-in-law thinks it strange that occasionally I neither wish to hear nor see too clearly—"

"Clearly!" Penndragon grimaced. "We have to shout at you and you bumble into furniture."

Ignoring him, she confided, "I find it a blessing to be shortsighted and hard of hearing. Makes the world easier to bear." She took a sip and continued, "But lately things are so interesting I feel no need to resort to silence and blurred outlines." She set her glass down violently. "Why always sherry? I *hate* sherry."

Grace had dressed for dinner. She wore a clinging tea gown that had seen better days and the hearing aid control was looped over a corsage of bedraggled artificial violets on one shoulder. Without the hat, she proved to have an unruly mop of salt-and-pepper hair cut into a Dutch bob. Directly over one eye another bunch of violets bobbed in her hair. As she perched on a chair between Forsythe and his secretary, Grace fell into silence. Miss Sanderson followed the older woman's intent gaze. Bunny was now seated at Susan's side on an ornate love seat. He'd thrown a casual arm over the back and one hand brushed her shapely shoulder. The girl

49

hadn't fussed over her dinner costume. She'd merely exchanged tight pants for a silk skirt and removed the artist's tam. She wore neither makeup nor jewelry, but with that face and hair, she needed no adornment.

As Miss Sanderson watched, Susan turned to Bunny and gave him a wan smile. Bunny whispered something and the smile widened into a laugh. Faint color stained her cheeks. She was amazingly lovely. Winslow Penndragon, Miss Sanderson noted, was watching the young people as intently as Grace and she, and with no evidence of pleasure.

"Bunny's good for her," Grace murmured and then said, "Poor child." Whether she was referring to her son or her niece wasn't clear. Grace raised her voice. "Observe Linda playing hostess."

Linda Evans had moved over to the hearth and was carrying on what seemed a one-sided conversation with Jason Cooper. He listened and occasionally nodded, which seemed his only contributions. "Like talking to the Sphinx," Grace told Miss Sanderson. The secretary silently agreed. Jason was a good-looking chap, but his father's description had been accurate. On that olive-skinned face was no trace of animation or expression. His half brother more than made up for his lack of gregariousness. Leslie Hobbs was not only talkative but positively garrulous. As he rattled on, he waved his hands and occasionally both arms. The object of his attentions was Winslow Penndragon. The older man made a gesture similar to that of shooing away a bumptious puppy and strolled across the room toward his daughter. Before he reached her, dinner was announced by a manservant.

He must be Linda's older brother, Miss Sanderson thought, uncle to the maids she had yet to see. There was no family resemblance between brother and sister. Evans was as tall as Linda was short, as gaunt as she was chubby, as formal in manner as she was chummy. An odd couple, Miss Sanderson thought, as she followed Linda and Penndragon down the hall—the housekeeper acting like a member of the family and the majordomo obviously keeping his place.

The dining room was similar to the other rooms at Penndragon—huge and smelling simultaneously of furniture polish, the fragrance from the floral centerpiece, and mildew. Evans and a plump little maid served a rather limp salad. Dolly—it had to be her because she was pretty—had a mass of dark curls and her uniform strained over a voluptuous figure. Winslow Penndragon seemed to be paying more attention to those swaying hips than he was to his salad. Examining the contents of her plate, Miss Sanderson didn't blame him. The only people doing justice to the first course were Jason, on her right, and Grace. Jason was chewing methodically and Grace as though she had no comprehension of taste or texture. Miss Sanderson concentrated on the wine, which was excellent. As Jason was making no effort to converse, she turned to the left, but Leslie, in a light shrill voice, was talking to Grace.

"—and so, Aunt Grace, I'm seriously considering having my name legally changed to Penndragon."

The woman's fork clattered to her plate and she directed the gleaming lenses of her glasses at the young man. "Really? Making a rather belated effort to legitimize yourself?"

"Of course not! As you well know, I am legitimate. But in my profession, Penndragon makes a better sounding surname. Can you imagine a restaurateur called Hobbs? Perfectly ghastly!"

"Hobbs *is* a ghastly name but I must admit it does suit *you*."

"Aunt Grace!"

Penndragon called, "Having trouble, Leslie?"

"Aunt Grace is being . . . she's frightfully rude to me."

"She's frightfully rude to everyone. Grace, do behave yourself." Grace made no response and her brother-in-law sighed. "She's turned off her hearing aid again. What's the use!"

Bunny remarked placidly, "Mother likes to have the last word."

"Unfair." Leslie turned to Miss Sanderson. "Don't you feel it *unfair*?"

Miss Sanderson was at a loss. She'd enjoyed the brief exchange and had a hunch Grace had taken the only course possible with Leslie. She hadn't really taken to him. Not only were his palms damp but beads of perspiration glistened on his brow. He was a compulsive talker and proceeded to regale her with a detailed description of his restaurant. "Miss Sanderson, my decorator knew instinctively the effect I sought—subdued elegance. A great deal of rich deep ruby velvet and dark wood. We used teak most effectively and . . ."

She heartily wished she had a hearing aid to switch off as his words continued to wash over her. Dolly and Evans served the next course—boiled mutton, boiled potatoes, and boiled cabbage. Blimey, she thought, and noticed both the host and Forsythe were helping themselves liberally to bread. She followed their example and tasted the wine Evans had just poured. Both wine and bread were first rate. A loaf of bread, a jug of wine, and thou . . . she wished fervently that Leslie Hobbs would shut up. He had exhausted his decor and was now working on his staff. "And my chef is French," he shrilled. "I'm certainly not a snob and didn't employ André because of that, but he is a *marvel*. I had to tempt him away from a *divine* little bistro on the Left Bank and . . ."

Frantically she tried to disassociate herself not only from that voice but her unappetizing plate. She caught snatches of conversation. Forsythe was chatting with a vivacious Linda; Bunny was engrossed with his lovely cousin; and Winslow Penndragon was odd man out. Susan had turned away from him to Bunny, and Jason, on Penndragon's left, was stolidly and silently addressing himself to a plate of boiled mutton. Leslie prattled on relentlessly, "One of André's specialties is Beef Richelieu. *Superb!* The Madeira sauce with just a soupçon of truffles . . ."

Practically salivating, Miss Sanderson reached hastily for a slice of bread. Surcease, she silently cried, help! I'm starving and this idiot is driving me bonkers. Help arrived from an unexpected source. A glowering Penndragon bent toward his daughter. "*Susan*, I've spoken to you twice. You're acting as deaf as your aunt."

Flaxen hair rippled across gray silk as she turned her head. "I'm sorry, Winnie—"

"That," Leslie blurted, "is not a proper way to address your father. Why can't you call him Daddy as I do?"

Penndragon's icy gray eyes fastened on Leslie's round face. "I like that term no better than Winnie." Having squelched his son, he said to Susan, "I was going to suggest you try a drop of this Chablis. It's quite distinctive."

"I don't drink."

"But surely a bit of wine . . ."

Eyes as gray and cold as his own locked with his. "You told me that before you approached us you had our backgrounds investigated. Surely you know *why* I don't drink."

"Your mother?"

"My mother was an . . . I could use the word alcoholic but, bluntly, she was a lush. Systematically and quite horribly, she drank herself to death. From my earliest memories, she was a zombie. Unkempt and hiding bottles and staggering—"

"My dear child, I wasn't suggesting—"

"The alcoholism was only a symptom of a deep-rooted illness. The illness was *you*. You used my mother as a toy and then threw her aside; she never got over you and spent her life drowning herself in drink. Father did his best and, as I grew older, I tried to help, but she slipped away from us. By the time she died I think we both were relieved to see her go. She put herself and us through hell."

"I had no idea," Penndragon muttered. "She married—"

"She married simply for Father's support—someone to look after us. The second time, Mother made a better choice of men. My father is—"

"Susan! Amos Vandervoort is doubtless an admirable

man, but he's *not* your father. I am your father. It's a bit late, but I fully intend to be your father. Please let me."

She laughed harshly. This time the laugh didn't increase her beauty. Her features were contorted, almost ugly. "*You*. You've not the slightest comprehension of fatherhood. You haven't the faintest comprehension of *love*. You've no idea what it is to love only once as my mother did."

Penndragon reached to take her hand, but she pulled away and sprang to her feet. "Being a father isn't only a biological act. Being a father is being *there*. My father was. He looked after me, kissed my bruises, played with me, let me help him put up the Christmas tree, went without in order to give to me." She stared down at Penndragon with open contempt. "After thirty years, you're trying to buy your children—with money. I don't know how Jason feels or even Leslie, but there's no price tag on me. I *have* a father and I don't want *you*." She dropped her napkin on the food congealing on her plate and bolted from the room.

Penndragon's face was as chalky as his daughter's had been. He pushed back his chair. "I'd better go after her."

"No," Bunny said firmly. "It would hardly be tactful. I'll settle her down." Throwing down his own napkin, he left the room.

Grace must have turned on her hearing aid, as she nodded her head until the violets bobbed up and down and said approvingly, "Really well done. Couldn't have done better myself."

"Aunt Grace!" Leslie protested. "Daddy, please don't be upset. Susan was perfectly horrid. She owes you an apology. Of all the ungrateful, *spiteful* girls!"

"Look, Hobbs or whatever your name is now," Grace rasped, "try not to be such a blithering idiot."

Leslie wailed, "Daddy!"

"It's seldom your aunt and I agree on anything, my boy. But right at present we do. Better take her advice." Penndragon turned to his other son. "We've heard from your sister and brother. What is your opinion, Jason?"

Jason shrugged. "She has a right to her opinion." His voice was deep and rich, but about as expressive as his face.

"I asked for yours."

"You're well aware of why I'm here."

"Indeed I am. Well, Leslie, it would appear you're my sole supporter."

"And a firm one, Daddy. I really admire you."

"Blithering idiot," Grace said succinctly and then, "I want dessert."

"Evans," her brother-in-law asked, "what delicacy is Mrs. Krugger regaling us with for a sweet?"

"Bread pudding, sir."

"Ye gods!" Penndragon rose with lithe grace. "Any who wish may remain and partake of Mrs. Krugger's pudding. For those who don't, coffee will be served in the drawing room." Belatedly, Penndragon remembered his newest guests. He spoke to Forsythe. "I should imagine you'll wish to retire. I'll walk you to the lift."

With the exception of Grace, there was a mass exodus. Linda Evans, chattering steadily with Jason, led the way. Penndragon followed, flanked by Forsythe and his secretary. Leslie trailed his father as closely as the retrievers had Bunny. When they reached the hall, Penndragon, with a weary but charming smile, said, "Rather a trying introduction, but it may be better tomorrow. Dinner was atrocious and if you wish I'll have Linda take up a snack for you."

"I had rather a lot of bread," Forsythe confessed. "And you were correct. Mrs. Krugger is quite a baker."

"Linda reports Mrs. Krugger's back is bothering her. If we're fortunate, she will take to her bed again. But regardless of that, I'll cook dinner for you tomorrow. Just a small group—"

"I'd love to taste your cooking, Daddy," Leslie chimed in.

"And you will—at a later date. Dinner tomorrow will be for Abigail and Robert and perhaps Bunny. We'll be discussing writing and you wouldn't be interested, my boy. Goodnight and sleep well." Penndragon took a couple of steps and halted. "Leslie, find Bunny and have those dogs detached from my door."

Helter and Skelter were still sprawled out on the threshold of Penndragon's tower. The male seemed to be dozing, but the bitch rolled her eyes and drew lips back from gleaming fangs.

"You don't care for dogs?" Forsythe asked.

"Not those two."

"Daddy," Leslie said eagerly. "I'll shoo them away."

"Go ahead and try," a voice said behind them. It was Grace, who must have finished her pudding at breakneck speed. "I'd love to see it, Hobbs. That bitch will have your arm." She paused beside her brother-in-law and peered up at him. "Winslow, I think you'd better speak to Bunny. He's paying too much attention to Susan."

"Do you want me to forbid him to associate with his cousin?"

"He certainly won't listen to *me*. And you know how I feel about cousins."

"Ah, yes—your Aunt Eunice." Chuckling, Penndragon told Forsythe and Miss Sanderson, "Grace's aunt married her cousin—"

"Laugh if you want, but their poor child—a congenital idiot!"

"How terrible," Leslie said. "Aunt Grace, I certainly do *not* approve of marriages between blood kin."

She spun around and glared at him. "If I didn't know better, I'd swear your parents were blood kin. If ever there was a congenital idiot, it's you."

His mouth snapped open, but she reached for her hearing control. As the lift door closed behind them, Miss Sanderson sighed with relief. "The end of a perfect day."

Later Miss Sanderson, attired in a flannel robe and a nest of hair rollers, checked on her employer. Forsythe was in bed with a heating pad draped across his bad knee. She adjusted the blankets and noticed how drawn his face was. "Anything I can get for you, Robby?"

"A whiskey is called for."

"You had rather a lot of wine with dinner."

"So did you."

"I'll make that two."

She handed him a glass, drew up a chair, and took a sip. "I hope Mrs. Krugger does take to her bed. If she doesn't, I'm going to be existing on bread. I wonder whether it's possible to get an overdose of starch."

"Let's have your impressions, Sandy."

She waved a hand. "Oodles. Jason seems a surly cuss. No, I take it back. Rather, he's completely self-contained. Susan's a stunner and Bunny, who looks like a nice doggy, is taken with her. Not that I blame him. But she looks ill and obviously hates her 'daddy's' intestines. As does the amazing Grace."

"Leslie Hobbs?"

"He's a . . . one moment, Robby. I'm thinking of the proper word." She poked at a roller and then smiled. "Leslie is a lickspittle."

"That does fit. I find I rather like Grace Penndragon."

"She has style and a tongue that makes mine sound kindly."

He drained his glass and handed it to her. "Tomorrow we go to work. We've seven principal suspects. I'll take three and because you're more mobile than I, you take the other four." He listed names and she made a face. "What's the problem?"

"Why did you stick me with Leslie Hobbs?"

"You were getting along famously at dinner, talking a mile a minute."

"Leslie was." She stood up. "Any instructions?"

"Proceed cautiously."

She laughed. "You try *that* with the amazing Grace."

Forsythe reached for the lamp. "I'll have her eating out of my hand."

"Want to make a bet?" Miss Sanderson asked as the light blinked off.

CHAPTER 6

THE MORNING ROOM AT PENNDRAGON PROVED TO BE MORE cheerful than the dining room. The paneling was washed in white and a pot of purple hyacinths sat on the breakfast table in a shower of weak but welcome sunlight. Grace Penndragon, clad in her dilapidated brown suit, and Susan Vandervoort, wearing a corduroy jumpsuit, were breakfasting when Forsythe and his secretary came down. The girl greeted them politely and Grace raised her head long enough to see who they were and then lowered it over a bowl of porridge.

"I'll get your plate," Miss Sanderson told her employer as he eased himself into a chair and propped his canes beside it.

Susan waved at the buffet. "Mrs. Krugger is still on her feet and the menu is a bit Spartan."

"I find it more than adequate." Pushing away her bowl, Grace neatly sliced the top off an egg. "Porridge and a boiled egg are a good way to start the day."

"The porridge is lumpy and the eggs are cold," Susan warned. "But the croissants are freshly baked and yummy."

Ignoring the other food, Miss Sanderson piled croissants

on two plates and poured coffee. "I'm still wondering whether one can overdose on starch."

"I haven't," Susan assured her. "And I've been here for a fortnight. Of course, Linda was cooking part of that time."

"You young people," Grace said disdainfully, "always complaining. As for you, Susan, you only pick at your food even when the incomparable Linda is cooking." She turned her attention to Miss Sanderson. "Somewhat of a celebrity, aren't you? Newspapers full of you last November—those mass murders in Maddersley-on-Mead."

Miss Sanderson was spreading marmalade and her hands abruptly stilled. "If you don't mind, I'd rather not discuss that."

"Sandy had a bad time," Forsythe explained.

"I suppose so. Probably quite different reading about it than living it. But you were quite a heroine, saving the child's life and all." Grace dug out a last fragment of egg. "But surely you can tell us how the little girl is now. What was her name? Lucinda Foster?"

"Little Lucy," Miss Sanderson said fondly. "She's coming along splendidly. Her uncle and aunt adopted her. They're fine people and have a girl and two boys of their own."

"Do you think you did Lucy a favor? Saving her life, I mean," Susan ventured.

Forsythe and Miss Sanderson stared at the girl. "I don't take your meaning," Forsythe said.

"I put it badly. What I meant was that Lucy Foster is only an infant now—"

"Thirteen months," Miss Sanderson said crisply.

"She'll grow older and when she does . . . think what a horror awaits her when she finds out what happened to her family. Sooner or later, she'll have to know."

The secretary was regarding the blond girl in an unfriendly way. "You think it would have been better to let a maniac hack her to pieces?"

59

"Of course not! I was thinking of the trauma the poor child will experience when she finds—"

"I think I know how Susan feels," Grace interrupted. She waved a hand. "This awful world! Full of bombs and unrest and terrorists killing innocent people. What a world for children to inherit. What a mess to bring them into."

The barrister arched his brows. "If people waited for a perfect time in history to have children, I fear the human race would have vanished centuries ago."

"Not a pleasant subject for breakfast," Susan said and rose. She said to Miss Sanderson, "I'm afraid I've offended you, but Grace is right. I was thinking along those lines." As she brushed past Forsythe's chair, she added, "I wonder whether the disappearance of our race would be such a bad idea."

He waited until the door closed and then he muttered, "She's awfully young to be so bitter."

"Not bitter," Grace said, "simply young and afraid and facing the death of a loved one. Death is not easy for the young to live with, Mr. Forsythe."

Neither is that girl's negative attitude, Miss Sanderson thought hotly. The barrister caught her eyes and jerked his head. She took the hint, drained her cup, and left him to Grace Penndragon. Forsythe found shortly that she was not going to be easy prey. She reached under her chair, found her string bag, and extracted the *Times*. Folding it at the crossword, she began, with remarkable speed, to fill it in. She used a pen and her printing was small and clear.

"I'm fond of puzzles too," Forsythe hazarded.

"Indeed? Then why don't you go and do one?"

"I'm strictly an amateur, but I can see you're an expert."

Heavy black brows drew together above the horn-rims. "Buttering me up, eh? The question is why. I'm very fond of *all* types of puzzles." She filled in more spaces and then the pen stilled. "You present no puzzle to me. You wish to interrogate me. Go ahead, it might be amusing."

"Why should I wish to interrogate you?"

"Come now. I may be old, but I'm not senile. Simply because I dress oddly and act oddly, people believe I'm dotty. The moment Winslow rang up from London and announced he'd be bringing you home, I knew his reasons. It's Forsythe the detective he wants, not Forsythe the eminent barrister and budding author. Wants you to save his miserable life, doesn't he?"

"Winslow and I *do* belong to the same club. I *am* writing a treatise on criminal law."

"And I'm the queen of the May. Posh! Don't insult my intelligence. My brother-in-law's had two narrow squeaks and, much to my delight, for the first time in his life feels what other mortals do—fear."

There seemed no sense in being evasive with this woman. Settling back, Forsythe charged his pipe and lit it, "What was the first?"

"When he smacked the Bentley into the embankment across the road. The second was when he narrowly escaped being beaned by that statue in the gardening shed. Nice tries, but he's tough to kill." The pen moved rapidly, filling in more spaces. "You're wondering how I know. Winslow covered up well and probably fooled the others, but I've time on my hands and I'm observant."

"The Bentley could have been an accident."

"Bullshivers! Winslow should never be allowed behind a wheel and I never drive with him. Evans is a dour devil, but if I need to go out, he's the one who drives. But even Winslow is not *that* inept."

"It could have been a mechanical failure, Mrs. Penndragon."

"If it had been, my brother-in-law would have fired his mechanic instead of turning the Bentley back to him for repairs. Anyway, Ed—he's the mechanic—spent far too long peering at the driveway in front of the door. When Ed left, I went out and found a damp area. I'd say it was brake fluid."

"Extremely discerning."

"Simple observation. The second attempt was rather risky. Poor old Jarvis might have gotten beaned with the statue instead of Winslow."

"Who told you about that?"

"Susan. Winslow has her convinced that it was Jarvis's carelessness. Jarvis is like me, old but still bright. Winslow swore him to silence, but I cornered him and he told me all about when he'd last entered the shed and so on. From there, it was simple to figure time and opportunity." She frowned thoughtfully. "A wonderfully complex puzzle. It will take more thought before I solve it."

She filled the last square and threw the paper on the floor. Forsythe picked it up and his eyes widened. "You *really* are the amazing Grace!"

"After the work I did during the war, that's mere child's play." She fished in her bag. "How would you like this?"

She held up the Argyle sock. Forsythe stared at the gaudy object. "*One* sock?"

She pointed at his cast. "Be a while before you can wear two. I made this for Bunny as a Christmas gift, but when I had the first sock done, I realized it was too small. Instead of unraveling it, I hung on to it."

He laughed. "Hoping to find a one-legged man?"

"A one-footed man." She waved it. "Pure wool and warm."

Taking it from her, he folded it and tucked it into his pocket. "I'm honored."

"Wear it in good health. If you solve this murder—"

"Attempted murder."

"—I'll knit the other one for you."

"Then you must help me."

She stroked her long upper lip. "I know I'm a suspect and I'm sure you'll want to know my motive. My motive is an emotion that surpasses hatred. I can't think of a word to describe my feelings for Winslow Maxwell Penndragon. It far transcends mere loathing. To understand, you'd first have to understand him. The image he presents to the world

62

is that of a devil-may-care, charming, daring man. And that is partly true. The other part, and this is carefully concealed, is that he's left a trail of victims behind him."

"You're thinking of the mothers of the three young people in this house."

"Sally and Joyce and Susan. Yes, and many others like them. Children, overawed at being seduced by this distinguished man. I'm also thinking of his comrades in the war, members of his own squadron who attempted to emulate his daring and lost their lives—"

"Come now! Fighter pilots were always in danger. You can't blame Winslow for their deaths."

"Ah, but I do." She passed a hand over her rumpled hair. "Mr. Forsythe, you didn't live through that war. You haven't the slightest conception of what a group of high-spirited young men, full of competitive spirit to be the bravest and most courageous, can be like. I know. My husband was one of them. Because of Winslow, his brother Gerald died. He was younger and had a case of hero worship for his older brother that was obsessive. Anything Winslow tried, Gerald had to have a go at. Winslow was a superb pilot; my husband barely competent. Winslow was well aware of this. He could have talked Gerald into enlisting in another branch of the service. He didn't bother. Gerald died. Winslow lived."

Her head drooped and Forsythe said softly, "The fortunes of war."

"No!" Her head snapped up. "Gerald was a *victim*. I am a victim. When he was killed, we'd been married barely six months. Winslow tried to prevent our marriage. Couldn't understand that his brother wanted an older, unpretty woman. But Gerald and I had something Winslow could never understand. We were deeply in love. I lost him forty years ago and I still love my boy husband. Forty years . . . alone."

"You have his son."

"Winslow has his son. Bunny not only looks like his

father, but he's like him in other ways. He worships his uncle. Bunny has lived in my brother-in-law's shadow—no life of his own. No relationship even with his mother. Bunny is also a victim."

"Winslow led me to understand it was Bunny's choice to stay with him."

"He had no choice. Winslow raised him . . . conditioned him. And now Winslow, on a whim, plans to disinherit him. Wouldn't you say I have an excellent motive to destroy this monster?"

"You've also given me one for your son."

She stood up. "Bunny is as capable of harming a hair on his idol's head as he is—" She halted and then thumped the crossword puzzle. "And Bunny is hopeless at puzzles." She stepped up to the buffet and tucked a couple of croissants into her bag. When she turned, she gave the barrister a brilliant smile.

He pulled himself up on his canes. "Mrs. Penndragon, will you help Sandy and me?"

"In what way?"

"Tell us about the rest of the household."

"No. I'll tell you only about myself."

"You don't want to prevent a third attempt?"

"I devoutly hope it will be a success. But I will tell you this." She opened the door. "If I'm your mysterious murderer, you'll not prevent my brother-in-law's death and you'll also never solve it. Mr. Forsythe, I'm very good at this sort of thing."

"And I, Mrs. Penndragon, am also very good at this sort of thing."

"You're a worthy adversary. My, but this is an exciting time! Haven't enjoyed myself as much in years. Now, get to work and earn that other sock."

The door closed. After a moment Forsythe pulled out the sock and thoughtfully looked down at it.

As she abandoned Forsythe to the mercies of Grace Penndragon, Miss Sanderson mulled over the four suspects that her employer had allotted to her. She decided to confront the least appetizing first and tracked down Leslie Hobbs. He was in the library, perched on a swivel chair behind an imposing desk. His dark eyes were roving around the room. With a great deal of dark wood and windows curtained in crimson velvet, the decor seemed to epitomize his idea of subdued luxury. When his eyes lighted on Miss Sanderson, he made no move to rise, but did make an inviting gesture at the chair opposite him. "Good morning," he said cheerfully. "Having a tour of Penndragon?"

"Looking around, yes. Your ancestors certainly built on a massive scale."

"They liked space and I inherited that from them. My restaurant—"

"You described it at dinner last evening."

"So I did. You know, I feel much at home here. Took to Penndragon immediately. Odd, because I've no background for a house like this. Mother and I always lived in rooms either behind or over our cafés."

"You seem to have taken to your father too. Was it a shock finding out about him?"

"In a way, it was traumatic meeting him. But ever since I can remember, Mother had told me all about him. We'd watch him on television or see a picture of him in a paper and Mother would say, 'He is your *father*.'" Leslie smiled and Miss Sanderson noticed a dimple in one cheek. He really wasn't a bad-looking man—short and pudgy and inclined to perspire readily, but he had nice eyes and an easy smile. He was also inclined to talk, and she settled back. It was soon apparent that Mother had not only told all about her romance with the dilettante but had built up hopes in her son of an eventual reconciliation.

"Mother would say," Leslie rattled on, "'Mark my words, one of these days your father will come looking for you. He never married and although he won't want me, I'm sure he'll want his son.' She was right, although she didn't live to witness it."

Miss Sanderson lit a cigarette. "Of course your mother had no idea that Winslow had other children."

"That came as a *shock*. Even when I arrived here, Daddy didn't let on about Jason and Susan. The next day, Jason arrived and Daddy introduced us and then to Susan when she arrived."

"Were Susan and your brother as surprised as you were?"

"I've no idea. At that point, I wasn't noticing anything but my own reaction. I felt strongly that Daddy should have told us before we got down here. Keeping us in the dark was unfair."

Unfair seemed to be Leslie's favorite word, but this time Miss Sanderson agreed with him. Not only unfair, she decided, but callous. Leslie had relapsed into a brooding silence, his full lips drawn into a pout. The secretary prompted, "And the three of you found you had a ready-made family."

"A father, a brother, a sister, an aunt, and a cousin. It was infernally awkward, but I made the best of it. I've done all I can to be agreeable to them. Jason and Susan ignore me—"

"Winslow told me about Jason's mother and Susan's stepfather."

"I guess you can hardly expect either of them to be overflowing with joie de vivre, but there's Aunt Grace. Every time I speak to her she says something incredibly insulting. Daddy says she's like that with everyone, but she isn't. She doesn't pick on Jason and she's nice to Susan."

"Your cousin seems a nice chap."

"He is. I get along like a house afire with Cousin Bunny, but he's not around much—always closed up in the tower with Daddy." The pout became more pronounced. "Do you know that I've been at Penndragon for a fortnight and not once has Daddy invited me into his quarters. He's had Jason and Susan in and tonight he's having you and Mr. Forsythe. Not *me*."

Before he could announce how unfair this was, Miss Sanderson hastened to say, "No doubt getting acquainted with his children one at a time. Your turn will come."

Leslie brightened and the words bubbled out. "Certainly it will! I'm simply nervy. You'd be too. Looking around at all this—" he made a sweeping gesture—"and not knowing if it will be mine or Susan's or Jason's." Bending forward, he said in a hoarse whisper, "Between you and me and the gatepost, I figure I've got the inside track. Jason doesn't even bother talking to Daddy and Susan—well, *you* heard her. That's no way to become Daddy's heir. Now, what I do is agree with everything he says, try to do little things for him. Show I'm *really* his son. I deserve to be his heir. Makes me see red when I think of what I've missed out on."

"Winslow said you'd had a normal childhood."

"Normal!" He spat the single word. "Being beaten by a drunken old bastard—sorry, Miss Sanderson, slipped out."

"Your father also said your stepfather was out of your life when you were six."

"Six years too late. He broke my leg, you see—in two places. Didn't heal properly. When I see Mr. Forsythe on those canes, I wince. Even now I limp when I'm tired. That sound like a normal childhood?" Without waiting for a response, he raced on. "Didn't get a proper education. Mother had me out of school at sixteen to work in her damn cafés—"

"You're still in the restaurant business."

"Restaurant. Not cheap little greasy spoons serving chips and fish, chips and steak, chips and eggs. A fine dining room with only the best food. No chips in *my* restaurant. And while I was growing up, Bunny was going to private schools, calling Penndragon home, traveling all over the world with *my* father. Wasn't that unfair?"

"Winslow seems to be trying to make amends."

"Sure. Giving us a little cash to get us here to decide which one *he* wants. Dangling us like puppets—" Leslie broke off abruptly and, apparently regretting his frankness, said quickly, "Don't get the wrong idea, Miss Sanderson. I'd appreciate it if you wouldn't mention any of this to Daddy. It's just that I'm so——"

"Nervy." Standing up, Miss Sanderson smoothed down her skirt. "Never fear, Leslie; I certainly won't repeat any of this to Winslow."

Only to Robby, she thought, as she left the library.

Forsythe glanced into the drawing room but didn't see his quarry. As yet his search for Susan had been unfruitful. He'd stopped Linda Evans, but she knew no more about the girl's whereabouts than he did. He had better luck with Linda's niece. "Saw Miss Vandervoort putting her coat on, sir, about ten minutes ago," Dolly told him. "Said she was going out."

As Forsythe donned his own coat, he decided Dolly Morris really was an attractive little thing. She had her aunt's eyes and radiant smile. She was also a flirt and the sway of her hips looked rather deliberate.

He stepped out and found that although it was sunny, the breeze was cool and brisk. He hoped Susan hadn't wandered far and, to his relief, found her on a bench near a well-tended maze. She had an open book on her lap but was gazing off into space. As he hobbled toward her, her eyes focused, and she gave him a wan smile. "Braving the elements too, Mr. Forsythe?"

"A breath of fresh air seems in order. I can't walk far, but I wanted to get out for a time. May I join you or——" He pointed a cane at her book.

She closed it. "By all means."

He sank down beside her, propped his canes, and turned so he could read the printing on the cover. *The Collected Works of William Shakespeare*. "Ah, another admirer of the Bard."

"Admirer? I suppose in a way. The man scares me half to death. He has captured every human emotion in words."

"This scares you?"

She was wearing a fur jacket over her jumpsuit. Pulling the collar up around her slender neck, she said somberly, "'For I am sick and capable of fears. Oppressed with wrongs, and therefore full of fears.' A few words written so long ago and yet expressing exactly how I feel at this moment."

"Your father?" Forsythe asked gently.

"After breakfast this morning, I rang up the home. He's no worse, but they can offer no hope." A sheen of tears made her gray eyes brilliant. "Strange, one never associates death with a person as vital as Father. When he had his first stroke I felt . . . betrayed—as though he'd done something cruel to me. When he began to feel better, he had to comfort *me*. I clung to him and wept and he held me as though I were a child again. Now, I don't even have that." A single tear ran down an exquisite cheekbone. "He doesn't recognize me and he can't speak . . ." She fumbled in a pocket, came up empty-handed, and accepted Forsythe's handkerchief. She dabbed at her eyes. "Sorry, I've no right to burden you with my problems."

"There are times when all of us need comfort." He hesitated and then asked, "Don't you feel a measure of comfort from your family?"

"A new family and all complete strangers. Bunny's rather a dear, but I've known him only a short time. Jason . . . what's your impression of him?"

"He seems aloof."

"He is. Completely remote. Only here because of a deathbed promise. How does Leslie strike you?"

"'Sweet words, low-crookèd curtsies, and base spaniel fawning,'" the barrister quoted solemnly and then thought, by George, I'm attempting to impress this young woman.

She laughed and warm color tinged her cheeks. "I told you Shakespeare said it all. I shouldn't poke fun at my half brother, but he's so eager to win Winnie's approval and all he manages to do is irritate his dear daddy."

"There's also your aunt and Winslow."

"I find Grace somewhat . . . sinister. That sounds odd, doesn't it? But despite those clothes and mannerisms she's formidable. One feels Grace is always one jump ahead."

Remembering his recent interview with the lady, Forsythe nodded. "And Winslow?"

"How tactful you barristers are," she mocked. "Careful not to call him my father. Last evening you heard my outburst and that's the way I feel about him. Well, perhaps I wasn't entirely truthful." She turned the heavy book over in her hands, hands the same shape and only slightly smaller than Penndragon's. "Winnie really isn't responsible for my mother's addiction. Her parents and her grandparents were all heavy drinkers. It was an inherited weakness. Even if Winnie hadn't treated her so shabbily, Mother might have drowned herself in alcohol just the same. But he brings out the worst in me. Winnie seems so sure he'll get what he wants."

"And he wants you?"

"I think so. He seems to have no feeling for Jason, and Leslie . . . well, Winnie seems to despise the man. But I feel he's gradually moving in on me—trying to control, to *force* me to love him." She lifted a haughty chin. "I refuse to love him and he can't buy me."

"Which may be the reason for his attraction."

She laughed again. "The unattainable. If Leslie was brighter, he'd act the same way and then Winnie might want *him*." A gust of wind lifted her long hair and she shivered. "I'm getting chilled. Are you?"

"Teeth chattering."

She rose, handed him a cane, and retained the other. "Lean on me. I'll help you into the house."

She did, supporting him with a strength surprising for her lithe frame. Forsythe was glad of her help, enjoying the feel of her fur-clad arm, the smell of clover in her blowing hair. At the same time, he felt a stirring of anger. Treats me as though I'm her doddering grandfather, he thought, and I'm not much older than she. Of course, with this damn leg and halting gait I'm probably acting the part. She hung their coats in the entrance hall, gave him his other cane and a lingering smile, and then walked down the hall. Despite her feelings about Winslow Penndragon, she not only looked like him but moved with his exquisite grace.

Words came to the barrister and he murmured aloud, " 'Thy hyacinth hair, thy classic face, thy Naiad airs have brought me—' "

"Quoting again, are we?" Miss Sanderson rasped from behind him. "You've the same idiotic expression Bunny has when he's gazing on that fair maiden."

"I fail to see anything idiotic about admiring pure beauty."

She gave him an impish smile. " 'Beauty is but a flower which wrinkles will devour.' "

"Not true in Susan's case. Bone structure. Must remember her father is far from young and still makes *you* drool."

"I'll ignore that. Now, Robby, you've had quite enough gadding around. Into the lift and collapse in that recliner. I'll take our lunches up in a bit."

She steered him toward the lift with Forsythe protesting. "I haven't finished my list yet."

"Neither have I. Whom do you have left?"

"Bunny, and I may be able to catch him at the luncheon table."

She held back the grill. "Your work is done for now. Bunny and his uncle are closed up in the mysterious tower. Linda says they lunch there and apparently even the effervescent housekeeper doesn't dare disturb them at work."

Forsythe found he was glad to reach his room and put his leg up. When Miss Sanderson joined him, she was empty-handed. "Met Geneva in the kitchen and she's trotting the tray up."

"What's she like?"

"When Winslow called her plain, he was being kind. Geneva looks like her uncle—built like a plank and with a

71

slight cast in one eye." She chuckled. "That's one working girl who's safe from the master of the house. How did you make out with the amazing Grace?"

Pulling out the sock, he held it up. "She gave me this. If and when we solve her brother-in-law's eagerly awaited murder, she's promised its mate."

"An unusual gauntlet. She's tumbled to us?"

"Had it figured out before we arrived. She's convinced another attempt will be made on Penndragon and hopes this one will be successful. Warned me that if she's the killer, we'll never catch her."

"And she's the lady you were going to have eating out of your hand."

A tap sounded on the door and Miss Sanderson went to collect their lunch. As the meal was spread on the table, he asked, "What in hell is this?"

She peered into the bowl. "For a moment I thought it was Bubble and Squeak, but this mess has obviously been boiled. Better down it. You need your strength."

He tasted it and grimaced. "Ugh! Penndragon must be out of his mind."

"Not so. Simply abysmally selfish. Stays in his tower stuffing down goodies while his family and guests face this slop. Have a roll."

Pushing the bowl aside, Forsythe spread butter lavishly. While he nibbled, he gave her the details on his talk with Grace. When he'd finished, she shook a baffled head. "Let's pray she isn't the culprit. I had a hunch she was more than weird clothes and weirder behavior. I also have a hunch that's merely an act to irritate her brother-in-law."

He nodded. "Susan called her aunt sinister." He filled her in on his conversation with Penndragon's lovely daughter. "Not much we didn't already know."

"Except that Susan's well aware of her father's tenacity. I could tell the way he was looking at her yesterday that he's made up his mind to have her, come hell or high water."

"It may not work, Sandy. Penndragon may have met his match."

Putting a dish in front of him, she ordered, "Eat your prunes. Now, my turn to tell all. Leslie Hobbs, bless his avaricious little heart."

When she'd recounted their conversation, her employer nodded. She flipped a hand. "So, Robby, you see I didn't get any more from Leslie than you did from his sister. He's rather slimy and practically taking inventory of his inheritance, but there's something rather pathetic about him."

"Also the fact that he actively resents being shut out of his father's life for so long."

"Much as I hate using the word, it does seem unfair."

"Unfair to all three children. Who's next on your list?"

"I couldn't get to Jason Cooper this morning. Linda said he'd been out for an early walk and then went to his room to read. I'll have a try for him now." She stood up and passed a hand over her gray hair. "You've stuck me with beauts, Robby. I've no idea how to approach Jason."

"You're resourceful. Tuck that afghan over my knees, please. Might as well have a nap."

"Nice to be an invalid." She arranged the colorful afghan. "How would you suggest I approach Evans and Linda? Bolt into the servants' quarters and yell, 'Hey, which one of you tried to knock off your boss?'"

Settling back comfortably, he closed his eyes. "Keep in mind that the Evanses could have a couple of good reasons."

"Linda and Dolly? Possibly. But Penndragon may be a bit beyond pursuing nubile maids."

"I'm inclined to doubt it. I can think of a couple of quotations—"

"No, you don't!"

She slammed the door behind her and Forsythe grinned.

CHAPTER 7

MISS SANDERSON DECIDED TO USE THE STAIRS INSTEAD of the lift. When she reached the bottom, she turned toward the rear of the house where the kitchen and various offices were located. She had come up with the skeleton of a plan, an excuse to speak to the majordomo and his sister on their own ground. She found Evans in the butler's pantry, perched on a high stool, his head bent over a tea service he was polishing. When he saw her he started to slide off the stool, but she waved him back. "No, don't interrupt your work, Evans. I was wondering whether you'd seen Mr. Cooper."

"Not since I served luncheon, miss. Mr. Cooper made no mention of his plans for this afternoon. He may be walking. A great gentleman for exercise is Mr. Cooper." He rubbed a chamois across the curve of a sugar bowl and added, "My sister might know his whereabouts. She spends a great deal of time talking to Mr. Cooper."

Or at him, Miss Sanderson said silently. She leaned against the counter. To draw Evans out, a compliment might be in order. "I'm amazed how you keep this place in such splendid shape with only a small staff."

"We manage, miss." Apparently feeling this too abrupt, he said, "We have cleaners in weekly, miss, and they handle the heavy work."

"It must be difficult finding maids, though. Girls generally prefer jobs in cities."

74

"Not like it once was." Setting down the bowl, he started on the creamer. "When I was a young man, girls were only too eager to enter service. Now they think themselves too good. Think they're a cut above us because they work in factories."

"Your nieces don't seem to feel that way."

He held the creamer up to the light and critically examined it. It looked fine to Miss Sanderson, but he spotted something and dabbed more polish across a handle. "That's my sister's doing, miss. Molly is determined that her girls will follow her into service. Begged Linda and me to get them started, see to it they're properly trained."

More compliments, Miss Sanderson decided. "You're doing a wonderful job with the girls. Both Dolly and Geneva are most efficient. When the girls leave, what will you do for maids?"

He rubbed vigorously and this time the creamer must have met his standards because he set it aside and began on the ornate teapot. "There're a couple of widows in the village who are willing to work here. Neither of them will ever see fifty again, but they know their job. Trained when girls were taught to work."

Great. All she'd done so far was get a quick course on the old versus the new. She tried a different tack. "How long have you been at Penndragon?"

Setting the pot down, he scratched at thinning hair. "Let's see . . . twenty-one years on the first of August, miss."

"A long time in one place. My, you must have been very young."

"Not that young, miss. This was my third position—and the best. Mr. Penndragon is a good employer. Never orders, always asks politely. He's away a lot too. That makes it easier. Only Miss Grace around most of the time and she's no trouble. Only time guests are here is when Mr. Penndragon and Mr. Bunny are home."

A lonely life for Grace, Miss Sanderson thought. Spending so much time rattling around this place with only a few servants for company. She was about to prod Evans with more questions when he spoke first. "This was my sister's first position. Only a young girl Linda was, but she took to it right away. Of course, service runs in the family. Our dad was a butler and our mum a cook. All of us—I've four sisters—followed in their footsteps. Molly—she's the mother of Geneva and Dolly—is housekeeper for a family in Glasgow. Should have found a position for both girls there. Too much responsibility for Linda and me, seeing to the girls."

From what Miss Sanderson had seen of the curvaceous Dolly, she was inclined to agree. But there was nothing for her here but the history of the Evanses. The majordomo appeared to have lost interest in his polishing and before he could start reminiscing again, she said hastily, "Perhaps Linda knows where Mr. Cooper is."

He glanced at his watch. "By now Jarvis will have brought in the flowers. You'll find Linda in the plant room. Straight down the hall, miss, second door to the left."

She thanked him and went in search of his sister. The housekeeper was setting pink-and-white carnations into a crystal bowl. She flashed her cheerful smile and asked, "What brings you here, Miss Sanderson?"

"Trying to find Jason Cooper. We haven't had a chance to get acquainted."

"Lots of luck." Linda trilled with laughter. "He seems rather left out and I've tried to talk to him, but he hasn't much to say."

"Some people are naturally shy."

"And ill at ease. But Jason seems quite relaxed. Maybe quiet by nature."

"He must find it tedious here, time hanging on his hands."

"Jason seems to fill it. Does a great amount of walking and reads a lot. He plays billiards with Leslie and is always trying to corner Bunny for a set of tennis. Too bad Bunny's so busy with Mr. Penndragon. Jason plays chess too. The night he dined in the tower, I understand he had a game with his father."

76

I'm running out of conversation, Miss Sanderson thought. "Your centerpiece is lovely."

The housekeeper looked as critically at the flowers as her brother had at the silver. "Not much choice right now. Only these and daffodils. Bad time of year for hothouse flowers. Jarvis tries, but he's getting on and the grounds take time." She positioned the last carnation and glanced up at her companion. "This is for Mr. Penndragon's table and it must be perfect. I understand you're dining with him tonight."

"Robby and I are looking forward to it."

Laughter tinkled again. "After your dinner here last night, that doesn't surprise me. You'll find Mr. Penndragon an inspired cook. Oh, by the by, he's requested all of us to turn up for tea."

"Mrs. Krugger's tea?" Miss Sanderson asked dubiously.

"Special treat. Can't tell because I'm sworn to silence. Happens only once a year and Mrs. Krugger and Mr. Penndragon make quite a ceremony of it. All that's lacking is pipers to usher them in." Miss Sanderson moved toward the hall and Linda called, "Might as well use the rear door. Jason is probably hanging around the tennis court hoping Bunny will show up. He's out of luck. Mr. Penndragon and his nephew are hard at it."

"Is Winslow working on another book?"

"That's a secret too, but I rather think he is. Be sure to slip something warm on. The wind's nippy. If you like, you can borrow my cape. Doesn't look like much, but it's comfy. Hanging on the peg by the door."

Linda's cape proved to be a voluminous garment fashioned of houndstooth check. As Miss Sanderson stepped into the wind, she pulled the hood up over her head. The tennis court was only a few yards from the rear door and her quarry was leaning against the back of a wooden bench. Although he was wearing a heavy red-and-black cardigan, Jason was bareheaded. As the door banged shut, he looked up hopefully. "Haven't seen Bunny, have you?"

She shook her head and he grunted, "Probably still closed up in the tower. Do you play?"

"Not well and certainly not in this weather." She spread

her arms and the cape ballooned around her spare figure. "A bit awkward in this getup anyway."

He scowled. "Well, might as well walk." Without issuing an invitation for her company, he set off briskly along a path.

Curt, bordering on rude, but she couldn't afford sensitive feelings. She trotted to catch up and adjusted her steps to his long strides. Jason evinced no pleasure in her company, but she doggedly set out to make conversation. "Linda tells me you're a great man for exercise."

"Tennis and walking. I don't jog and certainly don't do pushups and that sort of rubbish."

They were passing the gardening shed and she would have liked to have slowed for a closer look, but Jason was setting a hectic pace. "What do you do in the winter when tennis is out?"

"I keep busy."

"How?"

He stopped abruptly and looked down at her. His eyes, she noticed, were the same shade of brown as his wiry hair. His brow, high-bridged nose, and jaw were shaped much like his father's. "Look, Miss Sanderson, are you actually interested or just babbling?"

Her cool blue eyes met his. "I don't *babble*. If I wasn't interested, I wouldn't ask."

"I suppose I should say sorry, but most people prattle on as though they're scared stiff of a lull." He started off again, but this time his strides were shorter. "In the winter, I read and play chess and pore over my stamp and coin collections. Mama played chess and approved of the reading and collecting because they're solitary pursuits. She didn't approve of my playing tennis or joining the billiard club, but I did anyway."

"Approve? Surely you're old enough to do as you wish."

"As long as Mama was alive, I never got beyond short pants. Not in her eyes."

Jason made no effort to conceal the bitterness he obviously felt. Grieving for Mama? He sounded more resentful than sorrowful. "Your mother must have found it difficult raising a boy alone."

He snapped at the bait. "She loved every minute of it. You may have met women like her—wants a child, but not the bother of a husband." He gave a barking laugh. "I think when Mr. Penndragon bolted, he did her a favor. In all those years she never once mentioned my father, who he was, where he was."

His heavy brows drew together and the olive-skinned face was tight and closed. I'm losing him, she thought. "It's none of my business—"

"When people say that, you can be damn sure they're about to stick their noses into *your* business."

Enough was enough. Stopping short, Miss Sanderson wheeled, and marched back toward the house. To hell with Jason Cooper! Robby could have him! A powerful grip on her arm halted her and swung her around. "Kindly take your hand off my *nosy* arm!"

"Arms can't be nosy," he told her, and for a moment he reminded her of Robby. It was something he might have said. "This time I *am* going to apologize. You seem not a bad sort and I've bitten your head off for no reason except . . . I suppose I'm a loner, Miss Sanderson. All I've ever had was work in the shop and a few hobbies."

"And Mama." She softened and said gently, "Many of us don't like our parents."

"I didn't like her, but I did love her. When her illness was diagnosed, I was frantic. I couldn't picture life without her. Oh, I knew what she did to me, what she'd made of me, but what would I do without her? Without someone to tell me what to wear, what to eat . . ."

This is more like it, Miss Sanderson thought happily. "Winslow mentioned that you did leave her."

"At her insistence. She knew she was dying and wanted to see me set up. Her dream had always been of having a good-size bookshop in London. In a way she was an ambitious woman, but I was her only ambition. So, at her urging, I went to the city to scout a location." At the memory, the impassive mask fell from his fine features and

79

they glowed. "It was like being set free from a prison and I rebelled. Everything Mama didn't approve of I did. I drank a bit, not a great deal, but some. Mama would never let me eat veal. Claimed it was too hard on my digestion. For three nights in a row I had veal." He laughed. "Mama was right. I had indigestion that I shudder to think about. But the freedom, the wonderful freedom!" He sobered. "Then I was called back to Mousehole. Mama was dying."

"And you met your father."

"I met a famous man who claimed to be my father. He'll always be Mr. Penndragon to me."

"You're here."

"I'm here only because of Mama. I kept my promise because it was her last wish. I said she was ambitious for me. She wanted me to have a London shop, to have support from a wealthy father. I want neither a father nor a London shop."

"You said you liked London."

"No. I said I liked the freedom. I have that freedom now. As soon as this interminable month is over, I'll go home."

"To Mousehole?"

"It's the only home I've ever had. I'm comfortable there."

"And you hate your father?"

"Worse than that. Hate is a hot emotion. I feel nothing for Mr. Penndragon and want nothing from him."

She waved a hand. "Not even this?"

His dark head shook. "Not even this. Let Leslie have it."

A hand touched Miss Sanderson's arm and she jumped and looked down. Grace Penndragon had noiselessly approached and was standing at her elbow. She wore the straw hat tied under her chin and was attired in an old Burberry several sizes too large. The shoulders sagged, the too long sleeves were folded back, exposing a ragged lining, and the hem drooped over rubber boots. The hand clutching Miss Sanderson's arm wore a large red mitten; the other hand, this one bare, clutched a half-eaten banana. "Charming place to pick for a tête-à-tête," Grace said jovially.

"Cold," Miss Sanderson said, and shivered.

"Miss Sanderson is chilled," Jason said. "Better see her back to the house." He strode away from them.

"Unsociable chap," Grace said. "Noticed you'd softened him up some. Talking a blue streak. Some terribly reticent people do that when the right button is pushed. Dig up any dirt?"

"I'm freezing." The secretary set off toward the house. Grace tagged along and this time Miss Sanderson found it was she who had to shorten her stride to accommodate the older woman's gait.

"Being a Sphinx yourself, eh? Come on, loosen up. What did you learn from the lad?"

"I learned Jason Cooper has had one hell of a life."

"Lot of that going around. Mine's been no picnic. Where's the head honcho?"

"Honcho?"

"The boss. The great detective."

"Napping."

"In a warm room while you're doing the cold spadework."

"Mrs. Penndragon, where did you pick up these expressions?"

"You can call me Grace. Might as well. We've got a lot in common." Grace pushed the glasses up on her short nose. "Had a wonderful time adding those words to my vocabulary—during the war, from a strapping marine corporal. Built like a god, but with nothing between his ears but space. That was before I met Gerald." Her mouth quirked up. "It was a gas." She finished the banana, regarded the skin dubiously, and poked it down into her bag. "Care for a banana?"

"No, thanks."

"That's good. None left." She rummaged in the bag. "Ah, an apple." She bit into the fruit.

"I've been wondering where you got the Burberry."

"From a rubbish bin. It was Bunny's. Boy's horrible extravagant. Still a lot of wear in it, so I took it. Grew up in a poor family. Can't stand waste."

Miss Sanderson grinned. "I'll wager it's not waste you were thinking of but annoying your brother-in-law."

"Told you we had a lot in common. You're right. Every time Winslow sees me in this coat, smoke comes out of his ears. People may start to think his sister-in-law has to rummage in dustbins." The apple core followed the banana peel into the bag. "Winslow would dearly love to turf me out of his house."

"Turf? Honcho? I'd say your slang is more modern than the forties."

"Right again. Winslow can't abide slang."

"There's no need to ask what your favorite hobby is."

Grace laughed. "Bearbaiting or, in this case, Winslow-baiting."

Changing the subject, the secretary said, "I understand tea is a special event today. Do you know why?"

"Cherry brandy cake. One of the reasons Winslow keeps Mrs. Krugger on. A yearly ritual and he looks forward to it."

"There has to be *some* other reason."

Grace tilted her head back and, behind the thick lenses, her eyes looked sad. "Mrs. Krugger is all I have. When Bunny and Winslow are away, there're only servants for company. I can't abide Linda, and Evans is remarkably like Jason—another Sphinx. But Mrs. Krugger is sociable and it's pleasant to sit down with her for a cuppa and some chat."

Lonely, Miss Sanderson mused, so many desperately lonely people. Jason Cooper, who calls his father Mr. Penndragon . . . her thoughts veered to the Evanses. Odd siblings. Linda tossing off Christian names, Evans using only titles. Yet Linda always referred to her employer as "mister." Perhaps her hunch about their relationship was wrong.

"Hurry up," Grace urged. "Wouldn't want to miss tea."

CHAPTER 8

WITH THE EXCEPTION OF LINDA EVANS, THE ENTIRE household was gathered for tea. Forsythe, looking better rested, sat beside his secretary on the love seat. Behind the tea table, Penndragon was flanked by his daughter and Jason. Grace perched on a hassock and Bunny and Leslie Hobbs occupied opposite ends of a sofa.

Miss Sanderson muttered, "It's been ten minutes and my stomach's rumbling. Where's tea?"

"Methinks it's arriving," Forsythe told her.

Tea was arriving and the housekeeper had been correct. This was a ritual. Evans led the procession, solemnly bearing the gleaming tea service. At his heels was Dolly, dimpling over a silver cake plate. Miss Sanderson avidly checked the plate's contents. Only a small pile of tarts on one side. Hopefully she regarded the next person, but all Linda had to offer was a cake knife and a rather derisive smile. The last member of the procession was a middle-aged woman, pink and wide and comfortable, wearing a starched apron and balancing a pottery plate holding a rectangular object swathed in cheesecloth.

Evans deposited the tea service before his master, stepped back to a wall, and folded his arms. Lowering the cake plate, Dolly flashed a radiant smile at Penndragon. His hand rose as though to pat her enticing rump and then hastily pulled back. His housekeeper, losing her smile, dropped the knife with a clatter and thumped down between Leslie and Bunny.

Penndragon beamed up at the cook. "At this time, Mrs. Krugger generally says a few words. Mrs. Krugger?"

Turning even pinker, she cleared her throat. "Mr. Penndragon sets great store by this treat. Many's the time he's begged for the recipe, but it was my mum's and her mum's before her and, you might say, I have to keep it in the family."

Miss Sanderson's stomach rumbled audibly and she thought, get on with it and let's eat. The cook seemed in no rush. "This is a cherry cake and some might think that common, but I'm here to tell you this is no ordinary cake—"

"Hear, hear!" Penndragon enthused.

"Takes a lot of fussing and then it must wait. Take it too soon and it's mild, take it too late and it's gotten too strong." She tapped her bulging chest. "I know when it's just *right*!" She gazed around as though awaiting applause.

When none was forthcoming, her employer said genially, "Perhaps, Mrs. Krugger, you could unveil your treat."

Delicately she pulled back layer after layer of the mummy's wrapping. As the cake came into view, a strong odor of brandy wafted across the room. Mrs. Krugger reached for the knife, cut off a sliver, deposited it on a side dish, and with a flourish, handed it to her master. He took his time, first peering at it, then holding it to his nose and inhaling. The cook handed him a fork and he lifted a morsel to his lips. He appeared to be rolling it around in his mouth. Rather like a wine-tasting ceremony, Miss Sanderson decided. Mrs. Krugger seemed to be holding her breath. Then he beamed. "You've outdone yourself! There are no words!" Wreathed in smiles, the cook commenced slicing the cake and arranging it on the silver plate.

When she had finished, she stood back, her hands folded under her apron. Impatiently, Miss Sanderson waited for the cake to be served, but Penndragon was regarding the cook with open concern. "Linda tells me your back is acting up again."

"Indeed it is, sir. Agony I've had for two days!" A wide pink hand clasped her lower back.

"We certainly can't have that. You must go to bed immediately and put heat on it."

"Who will tend to dinner, sir?"

"Linda, you can cope, can't you?"

The housekeeper admitted she could and Mrs. Krugger said happily, "Good of you, sir. As I tell anyone willing to listen, Mr. Penndragon is a grand gentleman."

"Dolly, be good enough to help Mrs. Krugger to her room and see that she's made comfortable."

As the cook, leaning heavily on the maid's arm, departed, Miss Sanderson thought for a moment that the family would break into the round of applause the speech hadn't inspired. Penndragon swept an understanding look around the circle of bright faces. "That should take care of your stomachs for a few days. Now, my dear, will you hand around the cake while I pour?"

Linda jumped to her feet, but Penndragon was looking at his daughter. The housekeeper muttered and sank back. Susan, appearing unconscious of the honor just bestowed, handed the cake around. She took the plate first to Grace, who quickly snatched three slices, earning a glare from her brother-in-law. Linda, still looking like a thundercloud, took one small piece and Miss Sanderson, restraining herself, took two and a tart. After serving Bunny, Forsythe, and Leslie, Susan moved gracefully back to the table and placed the plate in front of her other brother. Jason reached for the side closest and took a couple of tarts. Penndragon deftly handed around cups and napkins and sank back into his chair. As he helped himself, he glanced at Jason's plate. "Jason, do have a slice of cake. I've no idea why those tarts were brought out. This is an occasion!"

His son swallowed and took a sip of tea. "Looks lovely, sir, but I'm afraid I can't have any. I'm allergic to cherries. Always have been. Break out in bumps."

"But you've had cherries since you've been here. I distinctly remember Linda serving an excellent cherry cobbler—"

"That was the day before Jason arrived," his house-keeper told him.

"So it was. What a shame."

Silence fell as they applied themselves to the treat. Lifting her fork, Miss Sanderson wondered what all the fuss was about. It looked like the cherry pound cake frequently baked by her Aggie. She tasted it and promptly changed her mind. Penndragon was regarding her quizzically. "Abigail, can you find a word?"

"Ambrosia," she breathed.

"Robert?"

"Definitely food for the gods."

Penndragon turned to his right. "And you, Susan?"

She put down her fork. "Too rich," she said flatly.

"Daddy," Leslie burbled, "my chef, André, could never match *this*."

For once he'd hit on target. His father gave a nod of approval and announced, "Anyone who wondered why Mrs. Krugger is at Penndragon now has the answer. Grace! What are you up to now?"

What his sister-in-law was up to was wrapping her last slice of cake in a tattered bit of paper. He glared at her. "You don't have to *steal* food!"

"Save, not steal." Giving a gamine grin, Grace stuck the package in her bag between the banana peel and the apple core. Then she minced toward the door, calling back, "Can you guess where the rest of the cake will end up, folks? First in the tower and then in Winslow's tummy."

"That woman!" Penndragon transferred enraged eyes from Grace to her son. "Your mother is the most . . . the *most* infuriating person I've ever known. At times, I think she should be certified."

Bunny told him mildly, "If you didn't react, she would stop doing it."

Penndragon relaxed and turned to the love seat. "Robert and Abigail, dinner will be served at eight, but please come at seven-thirty. Visitors are generally given a tour of the tower. Bunny will show you around, as I'll be busy in the kitchen."

As Forsythe and Miss Sanderson headed toward the lift, she told him, "If our host doesn't give us a hearty meal, I'm going to have to sneak down to the village. I'm desperate."

He laughed. "You're luckier than I am. I can't move well enough to sneak anywhere."

"Try raiding Grace's string bag."

"Cores and peels don't tempt me and I had sufficient cherry cake."

"Don't underestimate the lady. She could have a full-course meal tucked in there." As they walked toward their rooms, she said brightly, "Maybe Grace is trying to kill our dilettante with a stroke of apoplexy."

"I wouldn't put it past her." Forsythe added darkly, "In fact, I wouldn't put anything past Grace Penndragon."

When they returned to the entrance hall, they found Bunny, his dogs sprawled at his feet, lounging against the double doors. Skelter gave them her usual welcome, an ominous growl and bared teeth, but Helter didn't stir. Bunny glanced at his watch. "Right on the dot. Can't wait to see Uncle's domain, eh?"

"Can't wait to sample Uncle's cooking," Miss Sanderson retorted. "Penndragon would make a dandy clinic for weight reduction."

Bunny pushed open a door and then gazed raptly past their shoulders. They turned and saw Susan rounding the curve of the staircase. She moved in a drift of palest green and her lustrous hair was piled high on her head. No longer was her face chalky. Her cheeks glowed with color. Either she was feeling better or had resorted to makeup.

Bunny whispered, "'She walks in Beauty, like the night—'"

"Blimey!" Miss Sanderson pushed past him. "Another quoter."

Forsythe followed and Bunny hastened to catch up. The double doors led into a narrow hall that, in turn, led to another door. Bunny opened it, bowed, and ushered them into a circular area. Doors opened from it and a spiral staircase wound upward. The handrail was hung with charming bronze lamps.

"Main floor," Bunny said with an expansive gesture and then, like an elevator operator in a department store, announced, "Lounge, dining room, kitchen."

Forsythe steadied himself on his canes. "And this is the limit of my tour. I'll never make those steps."

"Not so. Over here, we have another lift, for the convenience of guests unwilling or unable to mount three floors on narrow steps."

"But not for the master," Forsythe said, hobbling into the lift.

"Perish the thought. Uncle, like his father before him, races up and down those steps like a mere lad. Next floor—mainly offices and a small art gallery. I'll give you a peek at the offices—unadorned working places." He threw open a door. "Mine."

"Oodles of the latest equipment," Miss Sanderson said enviously.

Forsythe pointed at a good-size computer. "Is all this necessary for writing?"

"Some of it, but writing is only a part of the work. My grandfather and great-grandfather bought up mines and textile mills and such, but Uncle Winslow, without expending any effort, has increased his inheritance manyfold."

"How?" Forsythe asked.

"Investing—an uncanny ability to know what to buy, when to sell. He's a financial genius."

Miss Sanderson lifted her brows. "With your help."

"He's the brains; I'm only the workhorse. Now, on to the gallery—a small collection but worth seeing." He opened another door, disclosing a hall-like area. Pictures hung on the walls, well-spaced and with a light beaming down on each frame. Both Forsythe and his secretary took deep breaths. The barrister said, "If I'm not mistaken, that's a Picasso."

Stepping closer to the painting, Miss Sanderson studied the acrobats depicted. "Circa 1905, his rose period."

88

Bunny's doggy eyes widened. "An expert, by Jove!"

"Hardly. When I was a slip of a girl, too poor to lunch out, in bad weather, I took my ham rolls to art galleries. While munching, I soaked up bits of information."

"Which she is more than willing to share," Forsythe said dryly. "Winslow really has catholic taste. Modern artists cheek by jowl with old masters." He halted before a large canvas. "Marvelous! The dappling of light across those shoulders—"

"Renoir," his secretary said smugly. "Circa—"

"Sandy!"

"I hate to cut this short," Bunny said, "but we must get on. If we're late, Uncle will be furious."

When they were back in the lift, Forsythe asked, "About security—"

"An alarm system on all the windows."

"What about all the doors?"

Bunny pushed back the grill and they stepped out again into the circular area. Here the staircase, in a shower of bronze lamps, ended. "Only one door into the tower, Mr. Forsythe, the one we entered from the main house. But not to worry. When Uncle's not in residence, his treasures are tucked away in a bank vault." He led them toward the only door opening on the round hall. "This floor has bedroom, bath, and dressing room—all fit for an emperor. Observe, Chinese Chippendale and trifles from all over the world."

The bedroom was indeed large enough for an emperor and, in keeping with the furnishings, the upholstery and walls glowed vibrantly in jewel tones. Looking at the crimsons, ambers, greens, and azure blues, Miss Sanderson thought them not dissimilar to Penndragon's vests. Bunny was leading her employer across an ancient silky rug toward a number of glass cases. "Uncle wants you to look at his jade. He said Adam Kepesake mentioned you collected."

"Nothing like this. I've only a few pieces." Forsythe pointed at a white jade camel. "Where did he get that?"

"Afghanistan. And this piece was from—" Bunny broke off and called, "Miss Sanderson, if jade isn't your cup of tea, do have a look at the cabinet of Meissen china."

"*This* is my cup of tea." She was standing beside the enormous bedstead. "Come look at these, Robby."

With obvious reluctance, he pulled himself away from the jade. His secretary was fingering a silver cherub on a pedestal by the bed. On the opposite side was another. Miss Sanderson's austere face was aglow with pleasure. "They look exactly like little Lucy!"

"They do a little—the ringlets, the dimples."

"A little! See the hands and those fat little feet." She lifted one cherub. "They're quite weighty. Look, Robby, one is standing, the other kneeling. Both the picture of little Lucy."

"With the exception of the wings, Sandy."

"Benvenuto Cellini," Bunny said with a grin. "Circa—"

"I don't care who made them or when. I *love* them. I covet them. I'm—"

"Hungry?" Bunny suggested. "Lady and gentleman, it is time. We've exactly three minutes to get to the table."

As they left the room, Miss Sanderson took a last look at the cherubim and sighed.

Winslow Penndragon's dining room was a dramatic contrast to the one in the main house. It was cosy, intimate, smelling only of carnations and the mouth-watering odors that wafted in each time the louvered door to the kitchen opened. Penndragon, with his nephew's help, handled the serving. The oval table was exquisite with candlelight gleaming on silver, crystal, and snowy linen, but Forsythe and Miss Sanderson reserved all their attention for the contents of their plates. As course after delicious course was served, little effort was made to converse. If Penndragon ever fell upon hard times, Miss Sanderson mused, he might well make a master chef.

It wasn't until they were having coffee in the lounge that she took time to observe their host. That evening he was wearing a sober black suit, a perfect foil for his choice of vests. This one was by far the most outrageous she had yet seen. All the colors of the spectrum were embroidered against scarlet silk.

Penndragon handed her a balloon glass. "I see you're admiring my vest."

"It goes well with the Chinese Chippendale. Should use it for a chair covering."

He laughed and his nephew said, "If Mother had said that, you'd be raging."

"Grace would have *tried* to be insulting. Abigail means it as a compliment."

Miss Sanderson hadn't meant it as a compliment, but she held her tongue. She could hardly insult a man who had just plied her with such a sumptuous meal. Striking a pose, Penndragon said, "I am now prepared to accept laudations."

Taking a sip of excellent brandy, she told him, "Tell you what. I'd swap both your Cellini cherubs for the recipe for that game pie."

"At times you *do* sound a bit like the amazing Grace. But not even for those treasures will you get the recipe. In confidence, I'll tell you this—be patient, purchase my forthcoming book and that recipe will be yours."

Her pale eyes widened. "You're writing a *cookbook*?"

He looked faintly chagrined. "Hardly that. Although this book does include my favorite recipes, each is accompanied by an amusing vignette of where and how I got it. It will be called *Delicacies for a Dilettante*." He turned to his nephew. "Remember the Sherpa village where we ate baked yak?"

"I would dearly like to forget it, but I must admit your version is delectable."

Miss Sanderson lit a cigarette. "I may pass on your book. Can't picture myself whipping around to my butcher for yak meat."

Penndragon sank into a chair beside her employer. "Robert, you're very quiet tonight."

"Hard to get a word in when Sandy gets going. But I would like to discuss your jade. You have a fantastic basket of fruit in three different jades . . ."

As Penndragon began to discourse learnedly on jade,

Miss Sanderson's attention wandered. She glanced around the lounge. Apparently the dilettante reserved his flamboyance for his vests and his bedroom. This room, like the offices on the first floor, was merely functional. There were no ornaments, but the chairs were comfortable, a gas fire beamed heat, and on the mantel above was what appeared to be an enlarged snapshot in a silver frame. Setting down her glass, she wandered over for a closer look. It had faded to sepia, but was still quite clear in detail. Beside the fuselage of a Spitfire, two young men posed. They wore flying jackets with sheepskin collars and their hair was blowing back from their faces. The taller man's arm was looped affectionately over the other's shoulders. Except for short hair, the tall man could have been Susan Vandervoort in pilot's clothing. "Uncle and my father," a voice said near her ear.

"I can see your resemblance to your father, Bunny. You have eyes and a mouth like his. But Susan . . . it's uncanny."

"Their mouths are different. Hers is more . . . more vulnerable."

She touched the glass. "I suppose these tiny rows of planes are—"

"The ones Uncle shot down. Impressive, isn't it? He was the ace of his squadron."

"Odd name for a plane. Why did he choose it?"

"No idea. My father named his after a famous singer."

"Bunny," Penndragon called and they turned. "You've been hard at it all day. Better have some time for yourself."

Having dismissed his nephew, he was returning to his conversation with the barrister when Bunny interrupted. "Will you need me further tonight?"

"Hmm. Yes, you'd better check in later. Make it in an hour."

And that, Miss Sanderson thought wryly, is the time he's allocating to Robby and me.

"The call you want me to make to your editor?"

"That and a few other things."

Bunny paused in the doorway and Miss Sanderson saw him glance at his watch. Uncle was extremely punctual, she remembered. Penndragon refreshed their glasses and turned his attention to Forsythe. "At the risk of sounding impatient, I must ask about your progress."

Forsythe lifted his eyes to the older man's face. "I think we've decided that you're mistaken about one of your children being the culprit."

"I am seldom wrong. Tell me, what is your reasoning?"

"I spoke with your daughter; Sandy with both your sons. After tea, we discussed this thoroughly and agreed not one of them has a ghost of a motive. Leslie doesn't like your nephew being raised as a son while you ignored him, but it's clear he desperately needs your financial help."

"That I know only too well. And my death would cancel any hope he has for that. Jason?"

"He has no feeling for you one way or the other. And he has no plans for expanding his shop in Mousehole and no desire to have a larger one in the city. If Jason has reason for resentment, it's directed against his mother, not you."

"I told you Joyce was a possessive woman. Now, the most important one. After Susan's tantrum at dinner last evening, it's clear she blames me for her mother's drinking problem and possibly her death."

"Susan confessed to me that she was simply hitting out at you when she said that. Her mother, she's convinced, would have drunk anyway. It seems Susan Miller came from a line of alcoholics."

Penndragon fingered a brilliant embroidered peacock on his vest. "Susan may hate me because when she needed a father, I wasn't there."

"I think she thanks you for that. Sounds as though Amos Vandervoort was the best father a child could have."

Penndragon colored faintly, but all he said was, "That's a relief. I should hate to think of Susan trying to kill me."

No mention of how he would feel if it was either of his sons, Miss Sanderson noted. While their host was feeling relief, she rose and returned to the mantel. "Your plane had an intriguing name."

His silver head swung toward her. "The Pansy? I named it for my mother's parlor maid. The chaps in my squadron found the name hilarious."

"Pansy—the maid; I mean—she was another of your conquests?"

"The reverse. I was barely eleven when Pansy seduced me."

"Precocious lad, weren't you?"

"Enjoyed every minute of it."

"Winslow," the barrister said sharply. "We'd best make the most of the hour you've given us. Tell us about another servant—Linda Evans."

Penndragon's color deepened. "Ah, you know."

"Guessed. Why did you withhold this from us?"

"It was such a trifling matter."

"Trifling to seduce a sixteen-year-old child in your home with her brother working for you? She *was* sixteen, wasn't she?"

"Yes." Unabashed, Penndragon braced an arm on the mantel. "Linda was the reason I employed them. Evans did have good references, but Linda caught my eye. She was such a tempting morsel. I made no attempt to mislead her. Linda was only too eager to come to my bed, but before she did, I assured her there was no chance of marriage and that my infatuations were short-lived."

"How long did this one last?" Forsythe asked.

"I really can't recall. Perhaps about six months, no longer. I do tire of these little girls quickly." He treated Miss Sanderson to a brilliant smile but this time she made no response. Her expression was as cold and closed as Forsythe's. Her host made another effort. "These girls are not like you, Abigail. All body—no sparkling intellect." When this compliment fell flat, he spread his hands. "I suppose you consider me a cad. Are you judging me?"

"We're not here to judge," the barrister told him. "Your morals, except as a motive for murder, are not of the essence. To return to Linda Evans. After you were through with her, she stayed on. Explain."

"When we were finished with our little affair—"

"When you discarded her," Miss Sanderson said flatly.

"When I discarded her, I gave her a gift of money and told her she might leave if she wished. She begged to stay on. I cautioned her she must not have false hopes. If she stayed, she would be a servant and nothing else and must act like one. The only concession I made was that she could join family and guests for her meals. She's abided by the rules."

"And her brother stayed on too," Forsythe said. "What is his full name?"

"Roger Evans."

"Was Roger Evans aware of his sister's seduction?"

"I've no idea. I supposed he couldn't have helped but be." Penndragon made an impatient gesture. "This is ancient history. Neither Linda nor Evans would wait over twenty years to take vengeance."

"Dolly Morris," Forsythe said tersely.

"I haven't touched Dolly! Well . . ."

"Details."

"It sounds rather sordid but . . . well, Dolly is like Linda before she put on all that blubber. Simply delicious! And it really wasn't my fault. It was Linda who—"

"Just the details. No excuses."

Penndragon's lips set. "Don't take that tone with me!"

"Do you want our help or not?"

After a moment, the older man shrugged. "A maid is sent into the tower each day to dust and generally straighten up. All Evans is required to do here is to act as valet and prepare my room for the night. When the Morris sisters arrived, it was Dolly to whom Linda gave the duty here. I came upon the girl when she was bending over the bed, putting fresh linen on. One thing led to another; Dolly was willing, and we ended up sprawling across the bed. I was merely kissing and cuddling the girl when Linda walked in." Pausing, Penndragon gave the barrister an indignant look. "She didn't even knock! There was a frightful scene and Linda slapped her niece's face and ordered her out of the tower. I

95

was so angry that I almost gave Linda her notice on the spot, but I had second thoughts. She would be too hard to replace. So I calmed her down, explained that the reason for my attraction was Dolly's resemblance to her when she was a girl, and eventually Linda came around. Since then, she's done the work here herself and hasn't let me near her niece. In fact, she's sending Geneva and Dolly back to their mother at the end of this month." Penndragon's mouth drew down at the corners. "Linda watches me like a hawk."

"How sad," Miss Sanderson said insincerely.

The barrister was direct. "Excellent motive there for both Roger and Linda Evans. Now, about your sister-in-law—"

"Grace is scatty!"

"Grace happens to have a mind like a honed razor. If she's the one we're looking for, you're a dead man."

"I find that hard to swallow." One of Penndragon's shapely hands caressed his chin. "Mooching about in rags, practically eating from garbage bins . . . she does have reason to dislike me, though. I remember when she became engaged to Gerald—he was still in training at the time—she came to me and literally begged me to persuade my brother to give it up and enter another branch of the service. She mentioned ground crew." He laughed. "A Penndragon servicing planes. Ridiculous!"

"Was your brother a good pilot?"

"Gerald wasn't washed out in training, but no, his reflexes weren't the best and he took too many chances. Tried to be *too* daring. But it was Gerald's decision and that's what I told Grace."

Miss Sanderson's sharp chin jutted. "Another excellent motive."

"After forty years?"

"Hate has a tendency to grow. First you took her husband and then her son as your own."

"Bunny? The boy has always made his own decisions. I didn't *force* him to stay with me. Now that you've met my nephew, you'll agree he's the least likely of the lot."

"I wonder," Forsythe said softly. "Bunny is obviously in love with your daughter."

"Merely an infatuation. When I came to your chambers, I mentioned Bunny was smitten with Susan. It will pass."

"Would you welcome a marriage?"

"Certainly not."

"Because they're cousins?"

"Unlike Grace, I have no objection to cousins marrying. My great-uncle married a cousin and they had seven normal children. But I would never allow my daughter to marry Bunny."

"On what grounds would you oppose it?"

"Susan is *my* daughter. She will *never* be my nephew's wife."

Or anyone else's, Miss Sanderson thought hotly, if this man can prevent it. Aloud she asked, "Does Bunny know of your feelings?"

"We've never discussed it. I simply assumed . . . he's quite sensitive and would never oppose my wishes." Penndragon again stroked his chin, apparently lost in his own thoughts.

Forsythe's voice snapped him back. "When you first came to us, I had two suggestions—"

"Yes, and we decided to get to the bottom of this affair."

"I've come to the reluctant conclusion that that is impossible. I haven't the faintest idea who is trying to take your life. Now I must urge you to consider my second suggestion. Leave this house and get away from this group of people."

Stretching out a long hand, Penndragon tapped the silver picture frame. "I've endured much more; I'm not about to turn and run now."

"In that case, I'm afraid Sandy and I must leave you to take your chances alone."

"You can't do that! I won't *allow* you to."

To Miss Sanderson's delight, Forsythe said dryly, "You don't control *us*. Tomorrow we return to the city."

"Showing the yellow, eh?"

Color drained from the barrister's thin face until even his ears were white. Pulling himself to his feet, he drew his slender body up. His eyes locked with Penndragon's. "I'm no more a coward than you. But I do have more common sense. You don't need a detective. You need a bodyguard." A cane rapped against the cast. "Physically, I can't protect you."

Putting out a hand, Penndragon said penitently, "I spoke hastily and I apologize. Won't you reconsider?"

"No." Forsythe, with Miss Sanderson at his side, hobbled toward the door.

Winslow Penndragon called after them. "I'll have Bunny put a check in the mail."

Robert Forsythe told him stonily, "It will be returned."

When they reached the entrance hall of the main house, Miss Sanderson stepped over Helter and said, "Bravo! A pity Grace couldn't have been there. She'd have loved it. Penndragon must have a death wish. Closed up in this place with seven people, most of whom have well-earned reasons for finishing him off. Blimey!" As the lift moved upwards, she took a close look at her companion. He was still pallid and his mouth was pinched. "Can't figure myself out, Robby. Even after watching the charm and polish crumble, I'm still fascinated by that man. Must be reaching my dotage."

His mouth relaxed into a faint smile. "When we met him, you put it in a nutshell. Winslow Maxwell Penndragon can't be judged by ordinary standards."

"True." She added wistfully, "Maybe he still has a few of the cat's lives in reserve."

CHAPTER 9

DURING THE NIGHT, THE WEATHER TURNED BLUSTERY AND now gusts of wind lashed icy rain against the windowpanes of the morning room. As though to make up for the weather, the buffet was laden with the bountiful breakfast that Linda Evans had prepared. With her at the stove, the culinary standards at Penndragon had risen appreciably.

Heaping plates at the buffet, Miss Sanderson felt content on two counts. Many of her favorite foods, hot and tempting, were spread before her and also she'd just completed arrangements for a hired car. She lifted a kidney and Forsythe called, "Whoa! Your eyes are bigger than my stomach."

Paying no attention, she added blueberry muffins and carried the food to the table. Leslie and Jason were bending over plates as well filled as the ones she carried and their sister was pushing kedgeree around. Beside her, Grace Penndragon sipped coffee and worked at another puzzle. As Miss Sanderson forked up scrambled eggs, Grace glanced at her over her glasses. "Evans tells me you've ordered a car. Bored with country life?"

Forsythe shrugged. "Duty calls. We've received a brief that my juniors can't handle."

"Odd. I wasn't aware a call had come through to you."

"Aunt Grace, a *few* things may happen that you don't hear about," Leslie snapped pettishly. His dimpled smile wasn't in evidence and his mouth was drawn in petulant lines.

"Not many, Hobbs. *You* received a call last night. From your accountant, I believe. Bad news?"

His mouth snapped open, but one of Grace's hands rose warningly toward the hearing control and he subsided, mumbling. She glanced at the mantel clock. "Wonder where Bunny is? Generally he's bolted his breakfast by now so he can wait on his lord and master. Linda's late in sitting down, too."

At that moment Linda appeared in the doorway, one fat hand clasping the jamb. Her face was the color of the table linen. "Winslow . . ." She took two steps and stopped, her heavy body swaying.

Jason and Leslie jumped to their feet, but before they could reach her, she moaned and slumped in a heap on the floor. Hopping up, Grace rounded the table. "Don't do that, Hobbs. Don't prop her head up. Get her feet up. Susan, ring for Evans. What in tarnation is wrong with the woman?"

"She's fainted," Leslie explained. "And she said something about Daddy."

"We can see she's fainted. Ah, Evans. Bring brandy and make it quick." Without any evidence of interest, Evans glanced down at his sister and backed out of the room. "In the meantime . . ." Seizing a pitcher of water, Grace dashed it over the housekeeper.

"That's enough." Miss Sanderson caught the older woman's arm. "Her eyes are opening."

As Grace bent over the woman, a voice said from the doorway, "Uncle Winslow's dead."

Bunny leaned against the doorjamb too and his face was as white as the housekeeper's. Leslie let out a wail, *"Daddy!"*

Grace took the situation in hand. "Bunny, sit down

before you fall too. Jason, lift Linda into a chair. Evans, pour a good tot of that into your sister and give Mr. Bunny one too."

"Was it a heart attack?" Susan whispered.

"Murdered." Bunny collapsed into the nearest chair. Bracing his elbows on the table, he lowered his head into both hands.

"Brace up," his mother ordered. "Are you certain?"

"His head . . . his face . . . all battered . . ."

"With what?"

"One of the silver cherubim."

"God," Miss Sanderson whispered and then she felt Robby's arm around her shoulders.

Grace took over from Evans, who now seemed as shocked as the others. She poured brandy and passed it around. Miss Sanderson gulped hers. Bending over her son, Grace shook his shoulder none too gently. "Did you ring up the police?"

"Right after I told Linda."

"Then we may expect Inspector Davis. Winslow called him out here last winter for some vandalism on the grounds. Heavy florid man, nearing retirement, I should think." She tapped restless fingers against the table. "Colonel Blake will be ringing up the Yard for assistance—"

"You can't be certain of that," Forsythe said.

"You can bet your booties on it. Known the chief constable since he was a lad—great one for passing the buck. Winslow is—was—a public personage. Colonel Blake will take no chances. The boys from the Yard will be here. And that means Adam Kepesake."

"This time your guess is wrong," Forsythe told her decisively. "They won't allow him to become involved in this. Winslow was his godfather."

"I'm well aware of that. Known Adam since he was a lad too. Feels much the same about Winslow as Bunny does— hero worship. Take my word for it, Mr. Forsythe, the boy will be here."

Leslie was close to tears. "How can you be so cool? Don't you have any feelings, Aunt Grace?"

"Someone must keep their head, Hobbs. Now, we'd better plan strategy. Bunny, any idea of how long he's been dead? Feel his skin, test for rigor mortis?"

"Mother!" Bunny lifted his head and stared at his mother. "Please, don't be ghoulish."

"You're acting as idiotic as Hobbs." Her glasses swung around the room and the eyes behind those heavy lenses were serious. "Let me tell you a few facts. I know you're stunned, but the police won't be. Adam will be ripping this place and us apart. One of you is a murderer—"

"I disagree." Jason's deep voice cut across hers. "That tower is full of valuable objects. Mr. Penndragon was probably killed during a burglary attempt."

"And how did the burglar get in?"

"Through a door or window."

Forsythe shook his head. "Grace is right. The only door to the tower is the one from the entrance hall. No stranger could have gotten past those dogs." He swung around to the majordomo. "Were the doors and windows locked in the main house, Evans?"

"They were, sir. Last thing I do before I retire."

"What about the windows in the tower?" Jason asked.

Bunny sat up straighter. He said slowly, "An alarm system is attached to all the windows. Once triggered, it sounds not only in the tower but on every floor in this house."

"Maybe we slept through it," Leslie suggested.

Grace glared down at him. "I heard it tested. Have to be deaf not to hear it."

"And *you* are," Leslie said maliciously.

"There's nothing wrong with your hearing or anyone else's. Face it. It's one of us. Better get your alibis ready."

"I haven't an alibi," Leslie said. "I was in bed asleep."

"How do you know that, Hobbs? We've no idea when Winslow was murdered. Mr. Forsythe, do you agree?"

"It might be wise." The barrister glanced around the table. "Think back and try to recall where you were last evening, whom you were with, what you were doing. Times . . . that sort of thing."

Leslie turned on him. "What right have *you* to advise us? You were in this house too. You or your secretary could have murdered Daddy."

Putting a hand on his pudgy arm, Grace told him not unkindly, "You really are an ass, aren't you." The glasses turned toward Forsythe. "Time for truth telling. Miss Sanderson and Mr. Forsythe are the only people who are not under suspicion. They came here, at Winslow's request, to try to prevent exactly what has—"

"Mother!" Bunny pulled himself to his feet. "*What* are you talking about?"

"Two previous attempts on your uncle's life." There was a storm of protests and Grace lifted a majestic hand. "Mr. Forsythe."

"Robby," Miss Sanderson whispered. "Do you think this is the right time to—"

"Grace is right, Sandy." He gave her a reassuring smile. "No reason to conceal this any longer. Winslow did retain me to look into this affair. I see no harm in telling you about the attempts." He outlined the car crash and the incident at the gardening shed. As he talked, his secretary watched the faces of his attentive audience. Grace looked smug, her son baffled. As usual, Jason was inscrutable and Leslie outraged. Behind her, Evans leaned against the wall and Miss Sanderson couldn't see him, but his sister looked dazed. Susan's head was bent and her flaxen hair veiled her face.

When Forsythe had finished, Grace nodded approvingly. "Well put. All the facts and no conjecture. Now I think all of you realize the gravity of this situation."

Leslie jabbed a finger at the barrister. "Spies!"

"Brought in by your dear daddy," Grace reminded. The doorbell pealed and she said, "Evans, you stay here. I'll admit the police. Too soon for Adam, so that will be

Inspector Davis and his boys." With a dignity strange in such a scarecrow figure, she marched into the hall.

Her son looked after her. "I can't believe it. Never seen her act like this. So . . . so competent."

"I doubt that you ever really saw your mother clearly before now," Forsythe told him gravely.

Sounds drifted down the hall, the piping of Grace's voice, deeper male tones, and then a storm of growls and barks. Bunny leaped up and ran into the hall. Grace returned first, rubbing her hands together, and looking gratified. "Dogs took exception to the invasion of the tower. Had at old Dr. Hawes—he's the medical examiner—and nearly took a chunk out of him. Bunny and a constable are taking the mutts out to the kennel." She posted herself at the door and beckoned to Miss Sanderson. "Come and watch. Quite a sight."

Nothing like a murder to brighten up a dull life, Forsythe thought with grim amusement. He'd seen it all too often— the police, plain-clothed and uniformed, the scene-of-the-crime men, the medical examiner with his bulging bag, most of them bored and jaded by crime, but efficient, knowing their jobs. How the dilettante would have hated it—strangers in his cherished tower, pawing over his personal effects, stripping his body, poking and prying . . . But then he was beyond caring, beyond anything.

Forsythe glanced around. Most of the others were watching Sandy and Grace. The exceptions were Susan and the housekeeper. Soaked to the skin, Linda was trying to dry her hair and the front of her dress with napkins. Susan's head was still bent, her glorious locks still concealing her face. The barrister suddenly noticed he was now sitting apart from the rest of the household. Those closest to him had discreetly edged their chairs away. No longer were Sandy and he guests. Sliding down beside him, his secretary echoed his thoughts. "Spies and pariahs, Robby."

"Yes."

"And probably flaming nuisances to the county constabulary."

He made no answer. That remained to be seen. Time passed, the minutes ticking by ponderously. A more subdued Grace returned to her chair and patted Susan's wrist. Throwing back her hair, the girl gave her a weak smile. No one spoke. The only sounds were the shifting of feet, Evans changing position against the wall, the clink of a cup against a saucer. Bunny came back and silently took up a post near the majordomo.

Finally Leslie jumped to his feet and blurted, "No one's told us we have to stay in here. I'm damn well going up to my room." He was soon back, looking slightly sheepish. "Constable by the door asked us to remain in here until they can take what he called 'preliminary statements.' If you ask me, it's awfully high-handed!"

"No one asked you," Grace said wearily.

Sitting down, Leslie proceeded to sulk. After a time, he muttered, "Hope they take me first. Like to get it over with."

He didn't get his wish. Miss Sanderson and the barrister were called first. They followed the constable down the hall to the stately library, where Inspector Davis had set up headquarters. He was seated behind the desk and a constable had cleared a side table and was laying out notebooks and pencils. Davis fit Grace's description—heavy and florid—and looked old enough for retirement. Score one point for the amazing Grace, Forsythe thought. Inspector Davis was hearty. "Glad to meet you. The chief constable has called on the Yard and I was speaking with Chief Inspector Kepesake. He'll be here to take charge and he advised me to talk to you first. Told me you might be able to throw some light on this tragic affair."

Score two and three for the amazing Grace—the Yard and Adam Kepesake. Forsythe cleared his throat and told Davis all he knew. He spoke tersely, but he left nothing out from the moment Winslow Penndragon had entered his chambers until the conversation with him in the tower the previous evening. Davis nodded his big head a number of times, looked scandalized when he heard of the dilettante's three illegitimate children, disapproving about Linda Evans and Dolly Morris, and when the barrister had finished, completely relieved.

"I'll tell you frankly, Mr. Forsythe, I'm happy Colonel Blake called on the Yard. At the time I figured he was jumping the gun but . . ." He turned his head and spoke to the constable. "See that this is typed up and ready for the chaps from Central Bureau. Thank you, Mr. Forsythe; you've been most helpful."

Forsythe picked up his canes. "Any objection if we wait in our bedrooms, Inspector?"

"Probably be a good idea. Shouldn't imagine the family is very welcoming now that they know why you came here."

"Pariahs," Miss Sanderson muttered again. Forsythe asked, "Isn't it irregular to send a relative of the deceased to head an investigation?"

"Highly." Davis chuckled. "But, according to Colonel Blake, the chief inspector threatened to resign if he wasn't allowed to come." Sobering, he patted his sizable paunch. "Not a sound idea. Too close to the deceased to think clearly."

"Would you mind giving us a few details about Mr. Penndragon's death?"

Davis silently debated and then said slowly, "I see no harm in it. Chief Inspector Kepesake will tell you anyway. Haven't much yet, Mr. Forsythe. Medical examiner puts time of death shortly after one A.M. Be able to pin it down better when he gets the autopsy done. Cause of death— blows to the head with a silver figurine."

"The Cellini cherub," Miss Sanderson said softly. "Which one?"

"Huh? Oh, one on the right side of the bed. The one kind of kneeling. Murderer left it propped up on the dead man's chest. Macabre touch."

Forsythe frowned. "Blows. Any idea of how many blows?"

"Quite a number. Smashed his head and face in. Dr. Hawes says it was overkill. With an object that heavy, one blow would have done it. No sign of a struggle. Body was tucked up and even the pillows weren't disarranged. Must have been sound asleep."

"Any fingerprints on the cherub?"

"Smudges. A surface like that doesn't take clear ones. And the killer could have worn gloves."

"There would have been a great quantity of blood."

"Lab boys are checking that now. Going through the bedrooms and so on. That's why we're keeping the household in the morning room. Of course, the killer could have had time to get rid of bloodstained clothes. Anything else, Mr. Forsythe?"

Forsythe said there wasn't and thanked him. As they moved down the hall, they met Bunny trailed by a constable. He averted his face as they passed him, but his mother, posted in the doorway of the morning room, waved jauntily and held something up.

Miss Sanderson pushed back the grill. "Knitting needles?"

"The other sock—a challenge."

"Blimey! Adam is going to tear our hides off."

"Mine, Sandy. And this time with some reason. His godfather was battered to death with me right in the house."

At his secretary's insistence, he lay down on his bed. He had thought he couldn't rest, but fell immediately into a deep sleep. When Miss Sanderson woke him, the room was shadowed and wind still gusted against the windows. Pushing himself up on an elbow, he switched on the bed lamp. Before he could ask, she said, "Nearly six. I went down to the kitchen and loaded a tray."

He swung his legs over the side of the bed. "I'm not hungry."

"Eat. You're going to need strength."

"I take it the Yard has arrived."

"Full contingent." She waved at a window. "I've been posted there. Adam and Beau and two uniforms. One of the uniforms looks familiar—that nice-looking chap from Adam's office."

"P. C. Helm." Forsythe bit into a sandwich. He chewed, swallowed, and said, "Maybe he'll leave us to last."

"And there are snowballs in hell. He'll want us first."

She was partially right. The summons arrived by Helm, looking solemn and distinctly nervous. But when Miss Sanderson tried to accompany the barrister, the young man shook his head. "Only Mr. Forsythe for now, Miss Sanderson."

Forsythe gave her a wintry smile. "Don't look downcast, Sandy. Your turn will come."

On the way down to the library, P. C. Helm spoke only once. "The chief inspector's pretty upset, sir."

What he means, Forsythe thought, is brace yourself, you're about to catch hell. Helm ushered him into the library, stepped in, and braced his wide shoulders against the door. Every lamp blazed and the light pitilessly exposed Kepesake's face. Lines were graven in that face that the barrister had never noticed before; the eyes were rimmed with red, the mouth set in a tight line. Even Kepesake's stance had altered. Generally he lounged back, his jade holder clasped between long fingers, smoke wreathing his head. Now he sat erect, his shoulders squared. No smoke drifted through the room and the cigarette holder wasn't in sight. Close beside him was Sergeant Brummell, and another, older constable sat at a side table, a notebook spread before him. On the blotter in front of Kepesake was a stack of typewritten pages, the edges neatly aligned.

The chief inspector started mildly enough with an inquiry about Forsythe's leg and an invitation to be seated. Then he brought his fist down sharply. "So that was my godfather's problem. Two attempts on his life! And I sent him to *you*. You stood by and let him be butchered!"

"Chief!" Brummell protested.

"No." Forsythe propped his canes against the desk. "Let him get it off his chest."

Kepesake's shoulders sagged and he fumbled in a pocket and pulled out the jade holder. "He gave me this. For a birthday. He gave me so much. Not only gifts. When I was a boy and visiting this house, he'd tell Bunny and me stories by the hour—where he'd been, what he'd done. To us he wasn't a man; he was a . . . a god. Larger than life, fearless . . ."

"I'm sorry, Adam," Forsythe said gently. "Sorry I couldn't save him." He touched his cast. "Helpless to protect him. But I tried—"

"I know. It's in your statement. I know you did all you could."

"He wouldn't leave here. He refused to listen."

"He couldn't. It wasn't in him." Pulling out a cigarette case, Kepesake inserted a white tube into his godfather's present. Brummell leaned forward with a lighter and Kepesake said brokenly, "At first I couldn't believe it. Couldn't picture him dead. Do you agree with the abolishment of the death penalty?"

Forsythe hesitated and then said, "Most of the time. Once in a while . . ."

"I'd like it reinstated. When I find the . . . the person who did this, I want him or her executed. I want him drawn and quartered. By God! I'm willing to do it myself."

"Chief," Brummell said again, "the superintendent was right. You shouldn't have come."

"It's the last thing I can do for him." Kepesake made a visible effort for control. "One shock after another. That statement of yours. I had no idea my godfather had fathered children—"

"No one did. Including two of those children."

"I didn't know he played around with teenage girls. It . . . it *tarnishes* him."

"That shouldn't diminish the man—his courage, his life,

his accomplishments. Sandy says quite rightly that Winslow Maxwell Penndragon can't be judged by ordinary standards."

After a time, Kepesake nodded. "She put it well." He glanced at the constable seated at the side table, pencil flying over the notebook. "Krimshaw! Don't be a bloody fool. Tear that up!"

Krimshaw flushed scarlet and hastened to obey. Brummell eyed him and said mildly, "I'll tell you when to start, Krimshaw." His bright blue eyes turned with open appeal to the barrister. "I've been trying to presuade the chief to let me take care of the household, leastways the ones he's close to."

"It's a sound idea," Forsythe approved.

Kepesake nibbled at his lower lip. "It will be awkward with Bunny and Aunt Grace. Bunny . . . well, we've grown apart, but when we were boys, we were close as most brothers. And I'm fond of Aunt Grace. She may act strange at times, but she's a kind woman. Always had sweets for us in her bag."

"A string bag?"

"No, then she had a cloth bag. Shabby affair, always bulging with odds and ends." Kepesake smiled slightly. "Quite a woman. She nearly drove Uncle Winslow mad at times." He added, "Aunt Grace will miss him."

Forsythe started. Then he thought that perhaps Kepesake might be right. After the excitement of her brother-in-law's murder had died down, Grace might well miss him. For forty years her spice of life had been annoying him. Old habits die hard.

Kepesake was staring off into space and Brummell was anxiously watching him. "Chief?"

Dragging himself to his feet, Kepesake tucked his holder in a vest pocket, and tried to smile. "I'll take your advice. I'm exhausted. You start the interviews, Beau. I'll be on deck in the morning."

"Helm," Brummell ordered, "find out which room the chief's been given."

The constable turned to obey, but Kepesake stopped him. "Same room I always have at Penndragon. Beside Bunny's. Beau, you'll be quartered in the one next to mine." On the threshold, he paused. "Robert." It was seldom he used the barrister's given name. "You'll help us, won't you?"

"Do you need to ask?"

"No."

Brummell watched the chief inspector leave and then he moved into the big chair just vacated. "After a night's sleep, the chief will be fine, Mr. Forsythe. He's badly shaken, that's all."

"Quite understandable," Forsythe agreed.

The sergeant riffled through the sheets on the blotter. "Any suggestion on who to start with?"

"You want me to sit in?"

"The chief asked for your help, sir, and so do I. Stay and ask any questions you want to."

"In that case, I suggest you have Mrs. Grace Penndragon in. As Sandy says, get the worst over first."

"Hard lady to get talking?"

"Hard lady to stop. A word of warning—don't let her clothes or eccentric behavior mislead you."

Glancing down at his rumpled suit, Brummell grinned. "Don't judge a book by its cover, eh? Helm, snap to it and bring in Mrs. Penndragon." He turned to look at the other constable. "As for you, Krimshaw, start your shorthand as soon as she opens her mouth. And if you're hot for a promotion, *never* do that again."

Krimshaw flushed again and his chin jutted. "Thought I was supposed to get it all down, Sergeant."

"Not when the chief's talking off the cuff." He got to his feet. "Mrs. Penndragon, please be seated. I'm Sergeant Brummell—"

"I know who you are. Asked your name when you arrived." She sat down and smiled broadly. "Saw Adam

111

going upstairs. Well, if you can't stand the heat, you shouldn't go into the kitchen."

It was Brummell's turn to redden. His mouth snapped open, but she was still talking. "Can't really blame the boy. Winslow filled his head with the same rubbish he did Bunny's. Boy's wasting his time grieving."

Giving Forsythe a wicked grin, Grace reached into her bag and took out steel knitting needles and a ball of emerald wool. Expertly, she began casting on stitches. "Little job I have to do, Sergeant. Don't fret. As Mr. Forsythe will tell you I can handle two things at one time. Now, on with the inquisition. I gave vital statistics to Inspector Davis. Want them again?"

"For the record, Mrs.—"

"Name, Grace Lillian Penndragon née Atkins. Age, seventy-one. Relation to deceased, sister-in-law, widow of Gerald Richard Penndragon. Length of residence in this house, forty years. Reaction to Winslow's death—immense satisfaction." She paused to watch Krimshaw's flying pencil and added, "No sense in asking whether I killed him. If I say no, you'll think I'm lying. Yes, and you'll think me mad. Carry on, Sergeant."

Valiantly, Brummell tried to carry on. "About the first attempt on Mr. Penndragon's life. Where—"

"Sound asleep in my bed. I'm not an early riser. Can't prove it." She bestowed her wicked grin on the sergeant. "Of course, I could have snuck down the backstairs, out the rear door, and diddled the brakes of the Bentley."

Brummell held out a sketch. "Could you point out the location of your bedroom?"

A needle tapped. "Here, beside the rear staircase, next to my son's—east wing. Same wing Mr. Forsythe and his secretary are in. Adam's room is next to Bunny's and you'll be here, Sergeant. My niece and nephews are in the west wing." The needles rose and stabbed at the younger constable. "You'll be in the servants' quarters. Better watch out for the pretty maid. Dolly is a looker and likes men, and you're a strapping lad."

Helm blushed to the roots of his fair hair and Forsythe said, "You mentioned that you're a late riser and yet for the last couple of mornings, you've been up before I was."

"That's because life started getting interesting. No sense in staying in bed when things are happening." Her glasses swung on Brummell. "Second attempt—I was on the same bench as Winslow, watching the tennis match. Not beside him. Never got too close to my brother-in-law. Evans was sitting between us."

Running a hand through his unruly hair, Brummell made another attempt. "If you'll give us a rundown on your movements—"

"—last night. Right." The needles flew and so did her tongue. "Linda Evans cooked dinner and everyone stayed at the table for pudding and coffee. Dolly and Evans served. We were five. My niece, my nephews, and Linda Evans. Jason and Hobbs left the dining room first—"

"Mr. Leslie Hobbs and Mr. Jason Cooper?"

"Right. The blithering idiot and the Sphinx. Said something about a game of billiards. Soon after, Linda left. Susan stayed on and we had a second cup of coffee. I had brandy too, but she never touches alcohol. Afterward—"

"Do you know the time you left the dining room?"

For the first time since she'd entered the room she hesitated. "Dinner was served at eight. It had to be after nine. I'm not certain how long."

Looking rather pleased at her hesitancy, Brummell asked, "Did you and Miss Vandervoort stay together?"

"For a time. We went directly to the morning room. I like that room and spend most of my time there. I was working on a puzzle and Susan went to the drawing room and brought back a book—Shakespeare. I'm rather knowledgeable on the Bard and we exchanged quotations. Susan's were rather morbid. She frets about her father—actually he's her stepfather—and after a time, I suggested she might better ring up the nursing home the old gentleman's in. She left and when she didn't return, I thought, poor child, the news couldn't have been good. I worked at my puzzle for a while and then I got bored and decided on bed—"

"Time?" Brummell asked.

"Before I left the room, I glanced at the mantel clock. It was eleven minutes after ten. I generally use the rear stairs, so I wandered down the hall toward them and met Evans and Hobbs. Evans was walking, but Hobbs was in a hurry. I'm curious, Sergeant, like to know what's going on. So I stopped Evans and asked what Hobbs' rush was. Evans said a call from his accountant in London had come in for him. I thought, more bad news, and then I went to bed."

"Directly?"

"Fast as I could." She held up a hand. "No, I heard nothing during the night. I'm a sound sleeper and I take this thing off when I retire." A needle flipped at the cord of her hearing aid. "Anything else?"

Brummell assured her there wasn't and thanked her.

Grinning at the barrister, Grace waved her knitting needles. An inch of sock dangled. She said jovially, "Our wager's still on."

As Helm closed the door behind her, Brummell asked, "What was *that* about?"

Forsythe told him and the sergeant shook a gloomy head. "Is her son anything like her?"

The barrister grinned. "Have him in and find out."

"Helm," the sergeant ordered. "Ask Mr. Winslow Penndragon to step in."

CHAPTER 10

BUNNY PENNDRAGON PROVED AS IMPASSIVE AS HIS COUSIN Jason and about as talkative. Ignoring the barrister, he gave his name, age, and relationship to the deceased in an unemotional voice.

The sergeant shuffled papers. "Would you be good enough to fill us in on your movements while your uncle breakfasted before the accident with his car."

As his uncle sat down, Bunny said that he'd left the table and had gone to his office in the tower. He put the papers his uncle required in a briefcase, took the case down to the entrance hall, and left it on the table there. Brummell selected a sketch and held it out. "I notice that from the windows in your office there's a clear view of the driveway directly in front of the main door. Did you notice the Bentley parked there?"

"I didn't go near either window. I was in a bit of a rush to get my uncle's papers ready. He hated to be kept waiting."

"And after you left his briefcase in the hall?"

"I went back to my office. I was typing the second chapter of his latest book, and he expected it to be done when he returned from Coventry."

"Were you surprised to hear of the accident?"

"Concerned about him, yes, but not surprised." Bunny smiled faintly. "There was a long-standing family joke about his driving ability. Uncle Winslow used to laugh about it himself. Said it was strange that such a superb pilot couldn't handle a car."

"You knew nothing about the previous murder attempts, sir?"

The young man glanced at Forsythe and then quickly away. "Not until my mother blurted it out this morning."

"Could you give us your movements last evening?"

"Mr. Forsythe has probably told you about the early part of the evening. I left the tower at twenty-six minutes after nine—"

"You're precise."

"Anyone dealing with my uncle had to be. When he asked me to return in an hour, he meant sixty minutes. I wandered down the hall, heard voices from the billiard room, and went in. Jason and Leslie were having a game. They're both good players and evenly matched, so I hung around and watched. They had some beer and I took a glass.

"Leslie won the game and Jason insisted on a rematch. At eight minutes past ten, Evans came in and told Leslie there was a call for him from London. Leslie hurried out and I stayed chatting with Jason until ten twenty-four. Then I returned to the tower. Mr. Forsythe and Miss Sanderson had left and Uncle Winslow was still in the lounge having a brandy. He gave instructions on a telephone call that I was to make to his editor and details on a couple of letters. When it was all clear, I said goodnight and left the lounge."

"And the tower?"

"No. I hadn't reached the doors that lead into the main house when my uncle called me back. He was in the central hall—"

"One moment." Brummell consulted another sketch. "That's where the spiral staircase is. Yes, go on."

The younger Penndragon had been speaking rapidly, but now he hesitated, cast a sidelong look at Forsythe, and said slowly, "The conversation we had has no bearing on this investigation."

Folding his hands over his stomach, Brummell said stolidly, "Let us be the judge of that, sir."

"It concerned Miss Vandervoort. My uncle asked me what my intentions were toward his daughter. Sounded like a line from one of those old melodramas and I was taken aback, but I told him the truth."

Bunny was hesitating again but Brummell didn't prod. After a few moments, the young man spoke. "I'm in love with Miss Vandervoort and I've proposed to her. Uncle Winslow asked whether she had accepted and I said she hadn't said yes, but then again she hadn't said no. He asked for details and I told him Susan—Miss Vandervoort—had told me that we hadn't known each other long enough to consider anything as serious as marriage. She also said she was too upset about her father's—her stepfather's—illness to think clearly."

"What was your uncle's reaction?" Forsythe asked.

Bunny didn't look away from the policeman and he did answer. "He was enraged. He told me I was a fool and to stay away from his daughter and to give up any idea of marrying her. I thought he must be joking and I . . . I'm afraid I laughed. Then he got really ugly. He said if I disobeyed, I could leave his house and he'd change his will and disinherit me. He said he would prevent our marriage no matter what steps he had to take."

"Did you lose your temper?" Brummell asked.

"Not at that point. I was stunned. My uncle had always been like a father to me and never in my life had he spoken to me like that. I asked him his reason and he said he'd his own plans for Susan and I had no part in them. Then I did become angry. I told him I was over forty and I would do as I damn well pleased. He gave me my notice—"

"Just like that?" the barrister asked.

This time Bunny's doggy eyes turned directly on Forsythe. "Just like that. Two weeks and I was to be out. Then he topped it by telling me I could take my 'insane mother' with me. That tore it and I fired back. I said all the things one says at a time like that. Told him neither Mother nor I had been charity cases, that I'd earned every penny for our support. It went on and on . . . accusations and counter-accusations."

"There were no witnesses to this?" Brummell asked.

"No. Well, there could have been one. While we were in the lounge, Evans had come in and Uncle gave him instructions—the usual, laying out clothes for the next day, drawing his bath, checking for clothes to be cleaned. While we were arguing, Evans was on the floor above."

"Could he have heard you?"

Bunny shrugged. "He might have caught some of it. We were speaking loudly, at times shouting. And the stairwell acts rather like a sound tunnel." His eyes were still fixed on the barrister. "Evans was the one who put a stop to our argument. He came down the steps carrying a couple of suits and a vest, and Uncle controlled himself and looked them over. He told Evans to have them cleaned and then he dismissed me. He said, 'That will be all' as though I was a servant, and I turned on my heel and followed Evans out."

"And then?" Brummell prompted.

"Another scene followed." Bunny's lips twisted and he looked even sadder than usual. "My cousin was waiting in the entrance hall of the main house and—"

"Which cousin?"

"Leslie Hobbs. He was as upset as I was. Said he must speak to his father at once. I tried to stop him, but he pushed past me and ran down the hall to the central core of the tower. My uncle was going up the stairs and he turned around." Bunny shook his head. "He was as brutal and ruthless with the poor chap as he'd been with me. Leslie tried to tell him about a call he'd just received from his accountant and Uncle cut him right off. Told Leslie no one ever entered his quarters without an invitation. He said Leslie would never be his heir." Bowing his head, Bunny looked down at his big hands. "Uncle told Leslie he would not give him any further financial help and he hoped . . . he hoped Leslie would lose his restaurant and everything else he valued. Then he ordered us out."

"And you went."

"We did. Leslie was thunderstruck and I had to take his arm and pull him back into the entrance hall. He tripped over Skelter, one of my dogs, and she nipped at him. The poor devil was in tears. I tried to console him, telling him to wait and catch his father in a better mood, that maybe he would reconsider."

Forsythe leaned forward. "Do you think he would have?"

"No."

"About you?"

"Uncle never changed his mind about anything. He meant every word he said to both of us."

The sergeant rustled papers. "What did you do then?"

"I went upstairs."

"To your room?"

"To the west wing and Susan." Bunny gave a twisted grin. "To pour out my woes. She had ample of her own. She'd rung through to check on her father and his condition had worsened. I begged her to leave this house with me and we'd both go to him, but she said she couldn't. She said Winslow Penndragon had bought a month and she knew he wouldn't release her from her promise. I blurted out . . . I proposed again and she repeated what she'd said before. Then I tried to embrace her—"

"Tried?" Forsythe asked.

"Susan doesn't seem . . . she doesn't like being touched. She was gentle and kind, but she said there was probably nothing for us and I should try to make it up with my uncle. I told her it was too late for that and then we said goodnight. I went to the east wing and to bed. I thought I wouldn't sleep, but I must have been exhausted. I fell into a deep sleep and . . . that covers it."

The barrister had been stuffing tobacco into the bowl of his pipe. Striking a match, he said, "Yet this morning you returned to the tower and your daily routine."

"I was forced to. Uncle had given me two weeks' notice and, frankly, I needed the salary. I've no savings and with Mother to provide for . . ."

Sergeant Brummell said briskly, "Tell us exactly what happened this morning."

"I followed my usual routine. At seven-thirty, I was at my desk. I opened some of the mail, took my uncle's personal letters and put them on the desk in his office, and then went down to the kitchen on the ground floor. At eight, I took a tray with tea and a roll up to his bedroom—"

"You did this every morning, sir?"

"Unless I was told otherwise. I found him and—"

"No need to go through that again, sir." Opening a folder, Brummell took out several glossy prints and handed them to Forsythe.

He studied them. They were taken from different angles, but all showed Winslow Penndragon's baroque bed and its grisly burden. The only way he could identify the face on the blood-soaked pillow was by the mane of silvery hair. Both arms were folded over the duvet and one hand touched the Cellini cherub. The innocent beauty of that little figure made the crushed and battered head almost unbearable. Forsythe's brow wrinkled. "Bunny, these papers and the folder on the bed—scattered all over the duvet—know anything about them?"

Bunny rubbed at his own brow. "They were reports on a couple of companies that Uncle was thinking of buying stock in. There were two folders. Stock quotations, graphs, management, that sort of thing. You'll notice one of the folders on the bed table. The other was just thrown around on the bed. Before you and Miss Sanderson arrived for dinner last evening, Uncle told me to put them in a drawer in his bedroom."

"Was Winslow in the habit of taking work to bed with him?"

"He did often. He didn't sleep soundly or for long. He said he liked to keep busy."

"Could he have dozed off while he was reading them?"

"I doubt it. He never had before. Every morning the work that he'd been looking over was always placed neatly on the bed table. Uncle Winslow was meticulous and loathed disorder."

Forsythe continued studying the prints while Brummell asked more questions. "Mr. Penndragon, are you your uncle's principal heir?"

"I am."

"He couldn't have changed his will without your knowledge?"

"No, he would have had me ring up his solicitor."

"Even if he was cutting you out of it?"

"Particularly if he was."

"It's a sizable estate?"

"Yes. Investments, property, book royalties, a recent contract for the film rights on his first book."

Momentarily the sergeant was diverted. "Will they be using the original title?"

"I believe so."

Brummell seemed to be mulling over a film entitled *How to Enjoy the Art of Dilettantism*. Bunny shifted restlessly and Brummell said, "That will be all for now, sir. Thank you for your cooperation."

Pulling himself up, Bunny wearily moved out of the room. Forsythe piled up the prints and placed them on a corner of the desk. He muttered, " 'Then felt I like some watcher of the skies/When a new planet swims into his ken.' "

"What's that supposed to mean?"

"Discovery, Sergeant. A belated discovery by Bunny Penndragon that his idol wasn't perfect."

Brummell's snort was similar to Miss Sanderson's. "None of us are."

"Ah, but we don't try to give the impression of

121

perfection. Winslow did. After forty years, his nephew finally saw him for what he was."

"Pretty heartless at that." Brummell darted a keen look at the younger man. "What do you suppose his plans were for his daughter?"

"Well, he was planning a clean sweep. With Grace and Bunny and Leslie Hobbs out of his life, there was only Jason Cooper left. And Penndragon was aware Jason would leave as soon as he could." Templing his long fingers, Forsythe gazed at them. "He wanted Susan Vandervoort all to himself—a vassal."

"The day he came to see the chief . . . Mr. Penndragon boasted that he always got what he wanted. If he'd lived, do you think he would have gotten Miss Vandervoort?"

Forsythe's answer was a shrug and Brummell called to the constable at the door. "Leslie Hobbs now, lad." He grinned at the barrister. "Better sit up and take notice."

"You have information on Hobbs?"

"A nice lot."

"This sounds rather fast, Beau. You only came on the case this morning."

"This is rather a special case. Inspector Davis, who's sharp, told the chief he thought Mr. Hobbs was hiding something and every available officer was turned loose on checking out his background. Shortly after we got here the report was phoned in. With that and what Inspector Davis discovered at the inn in the village . . . well, we have some ammunition to fire at Mr. Leslie Hobbs."

The sergeant held his ammunition in reserve. His approach to Leslie was slow paced and mild voiced. Forsythe watched the man assessing his interviewer, noted Leslie's initial uneasiness change to disdain, and was vastly amused. He was making the same error many others had with Brummell, judging the sergeant by his clothing and supremely ordinary face, and neglecting the sharply intelligent eyes in that face.

Brummell had worked around to the morning of the

second attempt on Penndragon's life. "You weren't with your father at the tennis court, Mr. Hobbs?"

"I'm not interested in the game." Leslie waited for the next question and when Brummell didn't speak, said, "I suppose you want to know where I was at that time. Sergeant, I'm going to be completely frank with you."

"Honesty is the best policy, sir." Brummell delivered the cliché guilelessly.

"I was in the tower." Leslie stared defiantly at the barrister. "*You* know how Daddy felt about his precious tower. One entered it only on his invitation. But I was curious . . . no, that's the wrong word. Meeting my father after thirty years and not really knowing what he was like . . . I thought if I could get a look at his quarters I would gain an understanding of him." Leslie's full lips drew into a pout. "And Daddy hadn't invited *me* to the tower. Susan dined with him and then Jason. Jason even played chess with him.

"That morning, I waited until Daddy had gone out to the garden and then, when I was certain the servants weren't in the tower, I slipped in." The pout disappeared and dark eyes glowed. "I'd only time for a quick look, but the *treasures*—paintings, collections of jade and china and antique silver—amazing!"

And all yours if you were to become his heir, Forsythe said silently. Brummell forged ahead. "Sir, kindly give us an account of your movements last night."

The memory of the treasures left Leslie's eyes. "A *terrible* evening. It started out not badly. For a change, dinner was palatable and afterward Jason and I played billiards. Jason *loves* games. I won the first game and Jason wanted to play another. Oh yes, Bunny joined us and watched and had some beer. We were setting up the table again when Evans came in and told me my accountant had rung up. I went to the nearest telephone, the one in the entrance hall, and met Aunt Grace wandering along the hall. She stopped Evans and I *knew* she would question him. Aunt Grace is incredibly nosy and I thought she might follow me and try to eavesdrop, but she didn't."

Perspiration was dewing Leslie's brow and he stopped to pull out a handkerchief and dab at it. Brummell was sitting back, his eyes half closed, looking as though he was dozing. Leslie rattled on. "Simply dreadful news. Floyd had been contacted by my bank manager—that man is *beastly*—and was told if I don't make payment on a loan in the next few days that the bank will take steps. *Steps*. They're going to foreclose on my restaurant!"

As though talking to himself, Leslie continued, "Everything I've worked for. My *life*. I knew there was only one hope—Daddy. But Bunny had said *you* were still with Daddy." He shot a hostile look in Forsythe's direction. "So I had to wait. I went back to the billiard room and tried to play. Jason became quite impatient with me because I couldn't keep my mind on the game. I tried to tell him about my problem, but he wasn't interested. I kept looking at my watch. Finally, I couldn't stand it any longer. I threw down my cue and *lunged* down the hall—"

"The time was?" Brummell asked sleepily.

"Exactly ten fifty when I reached the entrance hall. Jason had said Cousin Bunny was going back to speak with Daddy, so I had to hang around for another ten minutes before Bunny came out. Evans was with him and he had some clothes over his arm. I grabbed Bunny's arm and told him that I *had* to see Daddy. He tried to stop me and I went simply *wild*. I thought if I could just get to Daddy, he'd help. *Help*. Let me tell you—"

"Your cousin already has. Now, Mr. Hobbs, after you spoke with your father . . ."

"After?" Leslie blinked. "Well, I simply couldn't stand being alone. Cousin Bunny was kind, but he seemed upset too. He advised that I wait until my father cooled down and also said if he could, he'd help me himself. And I *knew* he would. Bunny's the only person in this whole house who's been decent to me. He went upstairs and I went back to the billiard room. Jason had racked up the cues, covered the table, and was piling beer bottles and glasses on a tray. Jason is *so* neat—a real mama's boy. He carried the tray to the kitchen and I tagged along. Linda Evans was there, heating something on the stove. Jason was hungry and he took cold meat and things out of the refrigerator. I had coffee and had to *choke* it down. When Jason had eaten, we went up to our bedrooms.''

Brummell stirred and slid a sketch over. "Kindly point out your room, sir."

"This one—in the west wing—down the hall from Jason. We said goodnight and I went along to my room. I couldn't settle down. I felt so alone. Not one of my relatives cared whether I was ruined.''

"With the exception of Cousin Bunny," Forsythe pointed out.

Shooting an unpleasant look at him, Leslie turned back to the sergeant. "I don't mind police," he told that worthy, "but I simply despise *spies*. Coming here and pretending to be a friend and snooping!"

Brummell's eyes snapped open. "Mr. Forsythe is here at my request and you will consider him my colleague."

"In that case, I suppose I've no choice."

Forsythe hid a grin and said, "You were feeling alone in your room."

"I went back to Jason's door and knocked. He seemed grumpy and when I asked him for one of his sleeping capsules, he—"

"How did you know about those capsules?" the sergeant asked.

"I saw the bottle a couple of days after we'd arrived here. We were playing a game of billiards and Jason fumbled in his pocket for something and pulled out a bottle of yellow capsules. He said that after his mother's death, the doctor had more or less forced them on him. I asked him what they were for and when he said he was going to get rid of them, I advised him to hold on to them. Never know when something like that will come in handy.''

Mopping at his damp brow, Leslie continued his grievances. "At first, Jason refused to let me have even one capsule. Said he didn't abide by drugs himself and didn't know how strong these were. Told me he doesn't believe people should pass around prescription drugs. I had to literally *beg* him before he opened the bottle and gave me one. I took it and . . . well, that's all."

"The sleeping capsule worked?" Brummell asked.

"Knocked me out like a light. This morning I felt pretty groggy, but it was worth it to get a good sleep."

Deciding the interview was concluded, Leslie took one last swipe at his brow, put his handkerchief away, and rose. Brummell waved him back. "Now, sir, if you'd tell me a bit about your restaurant." Leslie was only too eager to oblige. He was away in a flood of words about velvet and teak. Brummell shook his head. "Your staff, sir."

"Only the best, Sergeant. I'm like Daddy in that. The key positions are held by . . . well, André Marois is my chef. You may have heard the name. Widely known on the Continent . . ."

As Leslie chattered on, Brummell reached across the desk for a notebook. Flipping it open, he said, "You have a Spanish hostess and maître d'."

"Top notch. Lola Bianco and Cesar Guevarro. They—"

"They occupy the same flat, rather a lavish one."

"Nothing unusual about that, Sergeant, but in this case, not for the usual reasons. Cesar and Lola are cousins. And I do pay well."

"You're a frequent visitor to this flat, Mr. Hobbs."

"I am. Lola is my . . . I suppose you would say girl." Leslie considered and then added, "Mistress. If you could see her, you would understand. She's—"

"I haven't seen her, sir. But I understand Miss Bianco is a decorative young lady."

Leslie winked roguishly. "And a hot-blooded one, hot Spanish blood."

The sergeant didn't see the wink. He was consulting his notebook. "You give expensive gifts, Mr. Hobbs."

126

"With a beautiful creature like Lola, one must."

"What would a young lady like Miss Bianco want with a man's Rolex watch, expensive men's clothing—"

"I do buy a *few* things for myself."

Looking pointedly at the Patek on Leslie's plump wrist, the sergeant murmured, "Suits much too large for you. And—"

"This is none of *your* business." Leslie's upper lip now hung with drops of moisture.

The bright blue eyes snapped to the younger man's wet face. "In a case of this gravity, everything is *our* business. Another costly gift is a medallion, set with ruby and diamond chips forming the initials CG. Engraved on the reverse—'Leslie, with undying love.'"

Leslie looked as though he were melting away. Perspiration streamed down pudgy cheeks and his lips were quivering. Finally, he groaned. "All right, Sergeant. Lola only fronts for Cesar and me."

"Even the staff at your restaurant believes that Lola is your mistress. Why the secrecy?"

"You think I'm going to run around shouting, 'I'm gay and my maître d' is my lover'?"

"I see no harm in that. Society is most permissive now."

His head drooped and a bead of water fell unheeded from his nose. "Daddy."

"You thought your father would disapprove?"

"I knew he would. Mother used to say, 'Do what you want, but for God's sake do it *quietly*. Winslow would never stand for a son like *you*.'" He mopped his face off and then declared, "What am I so upset about? It makes no difference now. Daddy is dead. And *why* in hell should you care?"

"Your sexual preference is not my concern, Mr. Hobbs, but there happens to be a guest registered at the inn in the village—a young Spanish gentleman named Cesar Guevarro."

"I brought him down with me and dropped him off at the inn."

"You've visited him there?"

"As often as I could make an excuse to leave this house. Try to understand my position. I was coming to strangers and I'm *very* sensitive. I needed Cesar's support. Sergeant, we're in love. If it had been Lola, you wouldn't be so . . . so censorious."

"I'm not censorious, Mr. Hobbs; I'm merely doing my duty. I understand it's possible to take a shortcut from the inn to this property. There's a footbridge and rather a steep climb, but it would take only twenty minutes to reach this house and—"

"No!" Leslie was on his feet. He shoved his chair with such force that it teetered. Helm moved up behind him, but Brummell waved the constable back. "You're trying to frame us! You're saying Cesar fixed those brakes while I breakfasted with my— No!"

"Mr. Hobbs," the sergeant said mildly. "Get a grip on yourself."

"Motive? What possible motive could we have? Daddy was our last hope to save the restaurant."

"Your cousin seems sympathetic and he's your father's heir."

"Bunny?" Leslie lurched and grasped at the back of the chair. "I can't take any more. Can I . . . please let me leave."

"By all means, Mr. Hobbs."

Leslie stumbled toward the door and then turned. "I can't stay on in this house. Can I go down to the inn and Cesar?"

Brummell gave this some thought and then said genially, "I see no reason to keep you here. Helm, ask either Atkins or Richards to escort Mr. Hobbs to the inn. And, Mr. Hobbs, do stay put."

"I will," Leslie promised, and followed Helm into the hall.

Forsythe grinned. "You know how to fire ammunition, Beau, and you were also most understanding with Leslie."

"Understanding but not foolish. A couple of Inspector

Davis' boys are keeping an eye on Mr. Guevarro, and they can do the same with Mr. Hobbs." He glanced at his watch, a cheap one, not a Rolex or Patek. "Care for coffee?"

The barrister admitted it would hit the spot and when Helm returned, the sergeant sent him to rustle up coffee and biscuits. "On your way back, lad, ask Mr. Cooper to step in."

Helm shuffled his feet. "Sergeant . . ."

"Yes?"

"When I went for Mr. Hobbs, the young lady was looking pretty fagged. Like a ghost she was."

"In that case, bring Miss Vandervoort and better tell Mr. Cooper we won't need him until morning." Brummell grinned. "Mr. Forsythe, the age of chivalry is still lingering."

"With Miss Vandervoort, that ghostly appearance is not unusual."

"Good-looking girl, though. Any ideas stirring?"

"Early on, but yes—a few. You built a rather strong case against Leslie and the young Spaniard."

"In court, you'd be the first one to call it circumstantial." On blunt fingers, the sergeant rapidly ticked off points. "Mr. Guevarro made no effort to hide his identity, registered at the inn under his own name. The person who loosened that brake connection must have had some idea where the members of the household were. The gardener might have wandered around to the front of the house; someone could have looked out of a window or even come out. Seems foolhardy for a stranger to sneak onto the grounds and do it."

"True." Forsythe stroked his chin. "Winslow's bedclothes bother me—too neat. Beau, if a person was standing over you holding a blunt object and intent on murder, just what would you do?"

"Either jump up and grapple with him or roll to the other side of the bed. But Mr. Penndragon could have been attacked in his sleep."

"That doesn't square with what his nephew told us about Winslow's habits. And then, there's the murder weapon, the silver cherub. That bothers me too. It's such an awkward shape. Think how it would have to be held."

Swiveling his chair, Brummell looked searchingly at his companion. "It was handy, right beside the bed on a pedestal."

"Granted. But also in easy reach is a bookcase. If I remember correctly, it's used to display a silver collection. On the top is a pair of Georgian candlesticks—much easier objects to hold and swing."

While the sergeant was mulling this over, the door creaked open and Helm, wearing a smile and carrying a tray, solicitously ushered in Susan Vandervoort. Brummell gallantly seated her and hovered for a moment over her chair. Helm had been right. Susan was chalky and her dove gray eyes were deeply circled with dark shadows. Hollows showed under her cheekbones that Forsythe hadn't previously noticed.

Refusing coffee, she sat back, slender fingers fiddling with a gold chain belt. In a flat disinterested voice, she answered the preliminary questions. Brummell moved on to the attacks on the dilettante. "You breakfasted with your father on the morning of the car accident."

"Yes."

"And at the gardening shed, you called to him and saved his life."

"At the time, I had no idea I was saving his life. I simply wanted to call his attention to a clump of early blooming flowers."

"Didn't that whole affair strike you as strange?"

"Winnie explained that he'd asked the gardener to move the statue to make more room on the floor and quote 'The old fool had stuck it over the door' unquote. Winnie was so angry that I thought he'd probably discharge the poor old fellow."

"It's late, Miss Vandervoort, so we'll move on as quickly as we can. Tell me about last evening."

Susan told them much the same story as Grace Penndragon had. "I was thinking of phoning my father's nursing home and when Grace mentioned it, I decided to do it immediately. For privacy, I came here." She pointed to the telephone on the desk. "I was told my father's condition was deteriorating and the doctor only gives him a few more days." The girl's expression didn't change, but her fingers jerked at the gold links. "I had to be alone, so I went up to my room."

"You didn't consider appealing to Mr. Penndragon?"

A faint, ironic smile twitched at her pale lips. "Not for a moment, Sergeant."

"Why not?"

"Winnie was not a compassionate man. He'd paid for a month of my time and I knew he'd demand his pound of flesh."

"If you felt that way about him, why did you come here?"

"For five thousand pounds. I had to have the money to keep Father in the home. He gets the best of care there."

Brummell nodded. "And once in your room?"

"I paced for a while and then got ready for bed."

"You had a visitor?"

"Bunny Penndragon—for only a few moments. I take it he's told you about it." Brummell nodded again. "I felt sorry for him. He's been kind to me and so has his mother. It took me only a short time to see what Winnie was, but after forty years, it was a terrible blow to my cousin. Bunny was shattered."

"You refused to leave this house when he suggested it."

"I'd made a promise and I keep promises."

"How do you feel about your cousin?"

"That is *my* business. Your business is my movements last night. After Bunny left, I went to bed."

"Did you see or hear anything further?"

131

Her fine brows drew together in thought. "I saw nothing, but I did hear a few things. Nothing that could help you."

"Tell me anyway."

"Bunny had left my door slightly ajar and I hadn't noticed this until my half brothers came up. I was dozing, but their voices woke me. Jason's voice is deep and I couldn't hear what he said, but Leslie has a penetrating voice and I heard his every word. They said goodnight and then Jason's door closed—his room is across from mine. A few moments later so did Leslie's further down the hall. I was settling down again when a door banged open and someone started pounding. It was Leslie at Jason's door. He was demanding a sleeping capsule and even though I couldn't make out the words, I could tell Jason didn't want to give him one. I felt like shouting, 'For god's sake, let him have one so that we can *all* get some sleep.'"

"You don't care for Mr. Hobbs?"

A smile twitched at her lips again. "Grace has him pegged when she calls him a blithering idiot."

"Your feelings for Mr. Cooper?"

"At least he's quiet."

"Rather an odd reaction."

"Sergeant, try to put yourself in my place. Suddenly a father and aunt, a cousin, and two half brothers are sprung on one—some bearable and others—people you wouldn't bother with if you'd casually met them. And don't lecture about blood being thicker than water. A trite expression and I've no idea *what* it means."

"You have a point, Miss Vandervoort. After that interruption, did you go to sleep?"

"For a time. I should have gotten up and closed the door because I was roused again, this time by running water. It sounded like the shower in the bath. I thought, that blithering ass doesn't care whom he wakes up."

"That was all?"

"Yes."

Reaching out, Brummell poured coffee for the barrister

and then himself. Forsythe quietly asked, "Miss Vander-voort, have you any ideas concerning the murder of Mr. Penndragon?"

"None. To be brutally frank, I don't care. All I care about—" She appealed to the sergeant. "I must go to my father. He shouldn't . . . I can't let him die alone."

"I understand, miss."

"You've let Leslie leave. He stopped to tell Jason and me he was going."

"Only as far as the inn in the village. I haven't authority to let you return to London. But in the morning, I'll have a word with Chief Inspector Kepesake. I can't promise, but—"

"I'd appreciate it, Sergeant." She rose and bestowed a smile on him. This was no quick twitch, but Winslow Penn-dragon's brilliant, charming smile. She left the room with her father's lithe grace. Blood may not be thicker than water, Forsythe mused, but occasionally genes come through virtually intact.

"A troubled lady," Brummell muttered. "I'll speak to the chief."

"Sergeant." Ready color flooded into Helm's face. "I'd be willing to escort Miss Vandervoort to London."

"I'll bet you would, lad." Tilting back his chair, Brummell stretched his stocky frame. "That's all for tonight, Mr. Forsythe. We'll leave Mr. Cooper and the servants for the chief. No, not you, Krimshaw. Sit down and get to work. Get those notes typed up for the chief. Don't look glum, lad; you'll have help. Helm will give you a hand." He grinned at the good-looking constable. "Pretend Krimshaw is another maiden in distress. And, speaking of maidens, a word to the wise. Helm, that pretty maid bunking on the same floor as you happens to be sixteen."

"She looks older."

"Most girls do these days, but hands off."

"Miss Vandervoort has her outclassed, Sergeant."

133

"That's enough, Helm! Now, Mr. Forsythe, if you could point out my room."

They took the lift to the next floor and Brummell adjusted his steps to his companion's halting gait. Forsythe lifted a cane and pointed. "The last door is Grace's. The next is Bunny's and that will be Adam's. You're directly opposite." He swung open the door and found a switch. Jewel lights sprang up from shaded lamps.

Brummell gazed around. "My! Sure wish the wife could see *this*. Talk about how the other half lives. Funny, this is the first time I've ever stayed overnight in a house where we're investigating a crime."

"You may consider yourself fortunate, Beau. I've spent too many nights wondering whether a murderer is bunking in the next room. Little chilly fingers tracing a path up and down one's spine."

"I'd rather have stayed down at the inn. Think I'll lock the door. Goodnight, Mr. Forsythe."

Forsythe locked his own door, switched on the bathroom light, and hobbled across to his secretary's room. As he snapped the lock on her door, she called, "Who goes?"

"A burglar, Sandy."

Pushing up on an elbow, she switched on the bed lamp. Her head was a mass of plastic rollers bound in green chiffon. Under this bright helmet, her face looked longer and thinner. Blinking, she patted the duvet. "Sit, burglar, and tell all."

"Your thirst for gory details will have to wait. I'm beat, bushed, and completely bewildered and I'm off to bed."

"I will *not* be ignored like this. I'll get into the library tomorrow even if I must disguise myself as one of the suspects. Grace, I think. Turn out a ragbag and I'll be her doppelgänger."

CHAPTER 11

THE FOLLOWING MORNING, FORSYTHE WAS UP, BATHED, dressed, and on his way downstairs before his secretary stirred. It was shortly before seven and he didn't expect to see any of the household, but as he stepped out of the lift, Jason Cooper flung open the front door and came in. He wore a fawn raincoat and his dark hair and shoulders were drenched. Forsythe wondered what his reaction would be to the spy in their midst, but Jason was the same as usual. Flicking raindrops from his hair, he commented, "That wind has blown in a full-scale storm."

"Nasty morning for a walk."

"Have to have exercise no matter what the weather is like."

Jason brushed past Forsythe and headed toward the morning room. At a slower pace, Forsythe followed. He expected to find Brummell and the constables in the library, but a solitary figure was seated behind the desk, sleek head bent over a sheaf of papers. Kepesake lifted his head. "Didn't expect to see you so early. Leg giving problems?"

"Mainly the knee now. This infernal cast should be coming off shortly and that may make it more comfortable." Forsythe took a chair at the end of the desk. "Where's Beau?"

"Told him not to come down until eight. You worked late and Beau didn't sleep that well. Said it was the strange bed, but probably he was fretting about me. Like a mother hen, you know." Pulling out his holder, Kepesake stuck a cigarette in it. "And you can stop darting concerned glances at me, Forsythe. I was badly shaken yesterday, but I have myself in hand. Professionals have to, old boy. You amateurs have all the luck."

The barrister decided that the chief inspector was back to normal. Not only was he smoking heavily but he'd called Forsythe by his surname instead of the friendlier Robert and had also used the hated "old boy." Pulling out his pipe, Forsythe started scraping at the bowl with a penknife. "Have you had a chance to look over the interviews Beau did last night?"

"Was just finishing them when you came in. Beau left a note asking that I consider sending Miss Vandervoort to London and her stepfather. What are the details?" Forsythe outlined what the young woman had said and Kepesake nodded. "Compassionate grounds, eh? After I finish with Mr. Cooper and the staff, I'll give it some thought." His mouth set. "Beau has already allowed Mr. Hobbs to leave. Set a precedent that the others will try to use."

"Only to the village, and Beau had to come to an instant decision."

"He should have consulted me first. Well, at least Inspector Davis has the inn in hand."

Forsythe finished the small operation on his pipe and stuffed dark tobacco into its carved bowl. "Any results on the autopsy as yet?"

"One of Davis' lads brought it in a short time ago." Kepesake extracted a form and handed it across the desk.

Forsythe skipped over the first part. Description of Penndragon's general health, which appeared to have been remarkable for a man of his age. Winslow Penndragon

might well have made it to one hundred. Cause of death
. . . time of death, between one A.M. and two. He read on
to the marks and abrasions on the body—fading bruises on
the right upper arm and right hip. The car accident, he
decided. He read the next item twice. "Marks on both
shoulders?"

"Yes. According to the medical examiner, probably
inflicted shortly before death."

Handing the form back, the barrister said, "That answers
one important question."

"Which is?"

"Two people were involved."

"That we already knew."

"Surmised. Now we *know*. One person to hold him
down, one to use the cherub. But the bedclothes should
have been disarranged, kicking and so on. After the crime,
the bed must have been straightened, the arms arranged, the
cherub put on the victim's chest. Next question, any result
from the search for bloodstained clothing?"

"I had that yesterday. Neglected to mention it to you."

Forsythe's pipe clattered to the desk, spilling grains of
tobacco. "Mind sharing it now?"

"The country constabulary located it. A decrepit old
Burberry hanging from one of the pegs by the back door. It
was—"

"—used by Grace Penndragon," Forsythe chimed in,
remembering his secretary's description of that coat.

"Lab boys are working on it now. Cuffs and the front of
the coat were bloodstained. More stains on the mittens
found stuffed in a pocket of it—red wool with elastic cuffs.
Knitted by Aunt Grace and large enough to fit most hands,
unless they're paws like a gorilla."

"May be enlightening when the report is in on them."

Kepesake looked dour. "Don't get your hopes up. That
Burberry was a . . . I suppose you'd call it a communal
garment. It was originally Bunny's and when he discarded

137

it, Aunt Grace took it for her wardrobe—to annoy Uncle Winslow, of course."

"There's still five people left."

"A hair from one of his children or one of the servants? Afraid not. Aunt Grace was generous with that coat, offered it to anyone who desired it." Holding up a hand, Kepesake counted off. "Mr. Cooper borrowed it one rainy day rather than go up to his room for his own. Another blustery day, Aunt Grace insisted Miss Vandervoort wear it as she hadn't packed rain gear. Evans has admitted he frequently threw it over his shoulders when he went out to bring wood in and so on."

"That leaves Leslie Hobbs and Linda Evans."

"Linda often hung her cape over the Burberry when the pegs were crowded. One of her hairs could easily be explained. And Aunt Grace, who has a warped sense of humor, forced Mr. Hobbs to put it on. He was quite indignant. Said she made him look a fool. And that," the chief inspector said flatly, "is that."

"The mittens?"

"A splinter of nail polish, a flake of skin? Aunt Grace, Miss Vandervoort, and Linda don't wear nail polish. We'll have to await the report for anything further, but, frankly, I've little hope." Kepesake fitted another cigarette into his holder. "Forsythe, we're up against clever people. Using that Burberry was an inspired idea."

Forsythe, trying to light his pipe, nodded. It took time and four matches before he could add to the smog his companion had created.

Drumming restless fingers against the desk, Kepesake muttered, "Ever noticed how little one really knows about a person one's close to? I thought I knew my godfather as well as I know myself, but that isn't true. This man . . . this person those people spoke about is a stranger."

It was then that the barrister noticed Kepesake's recovery was far from complete. He had a grip on himself, but pain

138

lurked in his eyes and at the corners of his mouth. "You're thinking of Bunny Penndragon."

"He considered himself a son rather than a nephew. So did everyone else. How could Uncle Winslow turn on him like that? Forbid him to approach the girl he loves, order him from the only home he's known?"

"I think you must consider your godfather in a new light—human rather than a god. With human faults. A man who clearly loved only one person—himself. A man who would go to any lengths to achieve his own ends. He wanted domination over his daughter, and his nephew was expendable."

Crushing out his cigarette, Kepesake moved restlessly. "Looking back over the years . . . yes, there were signs. An old chauffeur who'd been with Uncle Winslow's father was thrown out because he dented the fender of a new car. I can remember Aunt Grace arguing, pleading with Uncle Winslow to let the man stay on. In vain.

"Later, there was a nasty business with the son of one of the maids. She was a widow and needed the work. Her son was older than Bunny and I and he was slightly retarded. He used to follow his mother from the village and sneak onto the grounds to play with us. He was a nice lad and we enjoyed playing with him, but when my godfather found out, he hit the roof. Said he wouldn't have a 'village idiot' associating with *his* nephew and godson. Ended up with the maid being sacked. The signs were there, but I was blinded to them. I suppose Bunny must have been too." The chief inspector pulled himself up short. "No sense in rehashing." The mantel clock chimed. "Eight. Beau will soon be with us. Ah, there you are. Right on the dot. Did you get any more sleep?"

"No, but I'm fine." Brummell, freshly shaved and wearing snowy linen, managed somehow to look as unkempt as ever. "Either of you had breakfast?"

The other men shook their heads and Kepesake said,

"Have it served in here. Less awkward. See to the lads, eh?"

"Helm and Krimshaw have seen to themselves, Chief. Packing it away in the kitchen. The cook, Mrs. Krugger, is still in bed. Planning on talking to her this morning, Chief?"

"It would be a waste of time. The woman seems to spend most of her time in bed. We'll have Mr. Cooper in first, then the servants."

Brummell nodded and went in search of breakfast. When he returned, he was carrying a loaded tray and was accompanied by Dolly Morris bearing another tray and managing her enticing wriggle at one and the same time. Kepesake pointed at a side table and the maid deposited the tray and started on her way out. Kepesake called her back. "Miss Morris, I've only a few questions for you. Perhaps you could answer them now."

Without waiting for an invitation, Dolly perched on the chair opposite the chief inspector. Forsythe noted that although she was striving to be demure, her skirt was hiked up, exposing dimpled knees, and extravagant eyelashes were fluttering at Kepesake. If she was hoping for a prolonged interview, she was to be disappointed. Rapidly, Kepesake elicited details of the evening of the murder. Dolly, with the aid of Uncle Roger, had cleared the dinner table and tidied the kitchen. Then she and her sister Geneva had been sent by their uncle to the servants' quarters. No, they hadn't gone straight to their own room. Aunt Linda had a telly and the girls watched the shows with their aunt until ten. "Then she sent us to bed," Dolly told them. "Treats us like kids, she does."

"And you heard or saw nothing further that night?"
"No."

She was now showing Kepesake more charming dimples, these in her cheeks. They made no visible impression on the chief inspector and he dismissed her, took his plate from the sergeant, and applied himself to bacon and eggs. Beau was

140

eating ravenously, but Forsythe took only toast and coffee. "Off your feed, sir?" Brummell asked.

"Not getting enough exercise," Forsythe told him.

Reaching for a rasher of bacon, Kepesake asked, "What about Helm, Beau? Any problem with him and that young hussy?"

"Not to worry. Sensible chap and I warned him off." The sergeant added ominously, "Better not be."

Forsythe recalled the good sergeant was the father of three children, two of them girls and pretty. Kepesake waited until Brummell had cleaned his plate for the second time and then told him, "Get this cleared away and tell Helm and Krimshaw to get in here. See whether Mr. Cooper's up."

"He's an early riser," Forsythe volunteered. "When I came down, I met him coming in from a walk."

As usual, Jason Cooper was completely expressionless. The chief inspector didn't waste time with him. He fired questions and Jason fired back answers. Neither of them used any unnecessary words.

"The morning of the car accident," Kepesake said. "You were out for a walk."

"I was."

"Did you go around to the front of the house?"

"No."

"Where did your walk take you?"

"Out the rear door, past the tennis court, to a lookout point over the village."

"You take that path every morning?"

"Yes."

"A creature of habit, Mr. Cooper."

"Yes."

"Your movements the evening of the murder."

Jason's account of the evening was exactly the same as Leslie's had been but much terser. He had played billiards with his half brother; Bunny had joined them for a time;

141

Leslie had been called to the telephone. "When Leslie returned," Jason said, "his game was off. There was no point in continuing and I told him so. He left again. While I was tidying up the room and putting the glasses and bottles on a tray, he—"

"You're neat, Mr. Cooper."

"Compulsively—early training."

"Continue."

"I took the tray to the kitchen and Leslie tagged along. I had a snack and then went up and he followed me. While I was undressing, he came banging at my door. He wanted a sleeping capsule and I gave him one."

"After some argument."

"I don't care for drugs, not even headache tablets. Mama didn't—" Jason broke off and then said, "I don't approve of people doping themselves, but Leslie insisted and he seemed in bad shape. To get rid of him, I gave him one."

"And then?"

"I went to bed."

"And to sleep?"

"Not immediately. Usually I'm a sound sleeper, but that night I twisted and turned."

"Why?"

"I've no idea. Leslie was so jumpy maybe some of it rubbed off."

"You didn't leave your room for the balance of the night?"

"Once. I thought a hot shower might be relaxing and I went to the bathroom and took one. Then I was able to sleep."

"What time was this?"

"I don't know. Late."

Forsythe leaned forward. "Did you see Mr. Hobbs take the sleeping capsule?"

"No. I handed it to him and closed the door."

Kepesake, who had been sitting bolt upright in his chair, leaned back and relaxed. He lit another cigarette, taking his

142

time. Forsythe's eyes shifted to Jason Cooper. The young man resembled the wooden Indian his father had likened him to. Since he had sat down, he hadn't moved once—no nervous mannerisms, no fidgeting. The only moving parts seemed to be his eyes and his lips. Yet he was a handsome man, a darker version of his father. The barrister had yet to see him smile. He found himself wondering whether Jason Cooper's smile had the charm and enveloping warmth of Winslow Penndragon's.

If the chief inspector was hoping to make the younger man nervous and more talkative, he wasn't successful. Jason simply waited patiently for the next question. Finally Kepesake asked it. This time his voice was different, softer and slower. "What were your relations with your father?"

"I had none."

"Could you enlarge on that."

"I came here because of a promise my mother had extracted. She was dying and I had to follow her wishes. I've simply waited for the month to end to return home."

"You weren't curious about your father?"

"No."

"What about the rest of your relatives?"

"The same applies to them."

"Surely not to your half brother and sister."

"Too little, too late."

Expelling a smoke ring, Kepesake regarded it. "A cold reaction, Mr. Cooper."

"Not when you consider the circumstances. Leslie, Susan, and I are over thirty. The only thing we have in common is that the same man sired us."

"And if you'd known of them earlier?"

"That would have made a difference." The wooden Indian suddenly showed emotion. Not in his face—that didn't change—but his voice roughened. "My life would be entirely different."

Forsythe tried to pin down the emotion in that voice.

Fury . . . sadness . . . despair? Kepesake asked smoothly, "In what way, Mr. Cooper?"

"I can't see where this has any bearing on your investigation."

"Let me be the judge of that."

"Very well. I've had a restrictive life. An overly possessive mother. As a result, I'm almost a recluse—no friends, few acquaintances. Mr. Penndragon could have told our mothers about each other. At least, he could have taken the time to let each of his children know about the other ones—their names, their addresses." Jason's eyes shifted, gazing moodily beyond his interrogator. "Years ago I would have been overjoyed to know that I had a brother and a sister. But Mr. Penndragon left it too late."

"And then only for his own reasons?"

"Exactly. He wanted nothing from Leslie or me. From the moment his daughter walked into this house, I realized she was his objective. Leslie and I were . . . we were window dressing."

"You held this against your father?"

"Not his choosing his daughter. That was his concern. But I'll never forgive his selfishness in not telling us of the other children he'd fathered."

"Perhaps he relied on your mothers to tell you who your father was."

Jason's mouth moved and Forsythe finally saw his smile. This smile bore no resemblance to his sire's. It was simply a grimace, lips pulling back from even white teeth. Remarkably like the wolfish snarl of Bunny's female retriever. It was fleeting and all emotion was gone from Jason's voice as he said, "Mr. Penndragon knew my mother, knew Mama would never tell me his name. She didn't want to share. Leslie's mother was obviously looking, as he is, for financial gain. That was her reason for telling her son about his famous daddy."

"And Miss Vandervoort?"

"I can only guess. From what she said one night at

144

dinner"—the dark eyes slid to the barrister—"it sounded as though her mother was too hurt and ill to ever broach that subject."

"So you put all the blame on your father."

"Wouldn't you?"

Kepesake said abruptly, "That will be all for now, Mr. Cooper."

The younger man didn't budge. "I should like to return to Mousehole. My shop is being looked after by an elderly clerk who's not terribly competent. I'm needed there."

"I understood you had sold that shop."

"I'd put it in the hands of an estate agency, but when Mother died, I changed my mind and took it off the market."

"As soon as the inquest is held, you'll be free to leave."

"Leslie already has."

Darting a cold look at his sergeant, Kepesake said, "Only as far as the inn in the village. If you wish to join him there, you may."

"I'm not that desperate." Jason left his chair and the room.

Swiveling his chair, Kepesake grated, "Never again release a suspect without my permission!"

"I was doing my best, Chief. I saw no harm—"

"You've put me in an untenable position!" Kepesake sank back and massaged his brow. "Sorry, Beau, put it down to nerves and to that Cooper. Cold as ice."

"More repressed than cold," Forsythe said mildly.

Kepesake glared at the younger constable lounging against the door. "Helm! Stop dreaming about Dolly Morris and get the Evanses in here."

Helm, blushing furiously, snapped to attention. "Sir, I wasn't—"

"On the double!"

"Yes, sir. Both of them, sir?"

"That's what I said."

Forsythe hadn't seen Linda Evans since the morning after

145

the murder. Then she had been sodden and dazed. She appeared to have recovered her high spirits and bounced in, her round face wreathed in a smile, followed by her gaunt brother. One hand was outstretched and she was talking. "Adam, my dear! Such a sad way to meet. It's been—"

"Miss Evans." Kepesake barely touched the plump hand. "As you know, I am heading the investigation into the death of your employer. Please be seated."

She dimpled at him as her niece had and with about as much effect. "Then it's Chief Inspector Kepesake, but I'll still think of you as Adam."

"Your thoughts are your own concern. Evans, do stop hovering and take a chair."

Evans lifted a chair over, placing it to one side and slightly behind his sister's. Crisply, Kepesake led them through the preliminaries. He spoke crisply to the major-domo. "After you delivered the Bentley the morning of the accident—did you enter the house?"

"Not immediately, sir. As instructed, I left the keys in the ignition and went around the house to the garage. As also instructed, I set out a number of traps there for mice."

"Is that one of your duties?"

"It certainly isn't," his sister said pertly. "Jarvis is supposed to take care of traps."

"Miss Evans, kindly bear in mind that I'm questioning your brother and I want his answers, *not* yours. Evans?"

"Jarvis usually attends to that sort of thing, sir. But Mr. Penndragon had noticed signs of vermin and asked me to look after it when I had brought back the Bentley."

"How long were you in the garage?"

"I really can't say, sir. When I entered the rear door, I found the house in turmoil. Mr. Penndragon was in the entrance hall and he was disheveled. Mr. Bunny wanted to send straightaway for the doctor, but the master ordered him to ring up the garage."

"At that time, you had no suspicion the accident had been a murder attempt?"

"I do my job, sir, and don't pry." Evans looked fixedly at the back of his sister's head.

"Admirable." Kepesake's eyes coldly examined the housekeeper. "Miss Evans, while the tennis game was in progress, where were you?"

"I don't really remember. I suppose in the tower straightening up."

"We have evidence you weren't in the tower at that time."

The dimples were no longer in evidence and a faint flush worked up her round cheeks. Her brother cleared his throat. "Beg pardon, sir. I believe Linda was in the plant room. At least that's where she was when I came in after the game was finished."

"That's right, Roger. Jarvis had brought the flowers in earlier than usual and I was arranging them. You must remember, Adam—Chief Inspector Kepesake—one of my duties is flower arrangement."

"Did anyone enter the plant room?"

"Let me see . . . so hard to remember. No, Geneva was upstairs tidying the bedrooms. Dolly . . . she was turning out the china cabinet in the dining room. I recall she didn't want to do it and I had to speak sharply to her." The dimples flashed again. "Mrs. Krugger, as Mr. Penndragon used to joke, was enjoying ill health and was in bed."

Kepesake shuffled papers, but it seemed only something to do with his hands. "Miss Evans, your movements the evening of murder from the time you left the dinner table."

She spoke as though she'd committed the details to memory. "As usual, Dolly and Roger cleared the table—"

"Your movements."

"All I was trying to say is that after dinner is finished, I go off duty. I went up to my room to watch television. Geneva and Dolly joined me and I let them watch a couple of shows and at ten sent them to bed. I'm very strict with my nieces. Another hour show came on and when it was over, I went down to the kitchen. I was heating milk for cocoa when Jason and Leslie came in. As soon as my drink was ready, I went up to my room, downed it, and went to bed."

"You saw or heard nothing through the night?"

"This is an old house, solidly built and sounds don't carry. Besides, I'm a sound sleeper."

Kepesake glanced over her head. "And you, Evans?"

"I'm on duty until dismissed by Mr. Penndragon. Dolly and I cleared the dinner table and tidied the kitchen. Then I sent my nieces to bed and started to lock up for the night. I checked all the doors and windows with the exception of the front door, which is left till last. I banked the fire in the drawing room and was going to do the same with the one in the morning room, but Miss Grace and Miss Vandervoort were in there. Then I returned to the kitchen to await Mr. Penndragon's summons. He rang for me at thirty-five minutes after ten—"

"You're a clock watcher?"

"In the evenings, sir. I'm getting on and my legs bother me—ankles swell. I went to the lounge in the tower and Mr. Penndragon gave me instructions—"

"Any that weren't usual?"

"Much the same as always, sir. It hardly seemed necessary to repeat them each evening, but the master did things his way. Mr. Bunny was in the lounge, getting his instructions for the following day. I went up to the next floor, turned back the bed, laid out night clothes, and started to run a bath. While the tub was filling, I looked over the wardrobe, found some clothing that needed cleaning, and later took them down for Mr. Penndragon's approval." A shade of expression crossed the dour features and Evans confided, "A stickler the master was for clothes, sir. Liked everything just so. Always looked a treat, he did."

"Yes," Kepesake said somberly. "While you went about your duties did you hear Mr. Penndragon and his nephew talking?"

Evans appeared to be debating and then he said slowly,

"No use in dodging, sir. Yes, I heard them. Couldn't help it. They were both shouting."

"And you got the gist of their quarrel?"

"It was about Miss Vandervoort. The master was telling Mr. Bunny to leave her alone. Ended up with Mr. Penndragon yelling that Mr. Bunny was through and he could get out and take Miss Grace with him. Terrible it was. I couldn't believe my ears."

Kepesake was restlessly toying with his jade holder. "Evans, I want a straight answer on this. Did you tell Mrs. Penndragon what you'd heard?"

"Well . . . I'll admit I would have if she'd been downstairs, but by the time I bolted the front door, she'd gone up."

"Fond of her, are you?"

"Think we all are, sir. Jarvis thinks the world of her."

"I'm certainly not," Linda blurted. "The way she dresses and talks—it's disgraceful!"

"Seeing that you want to answer questions so badly, Miss Evans, I have a few for you. Exactly what was your relationship with the deceased?"

She drew her thick body up. "As you well know, I was his housekeeper."

Her brother directed a broad grin at the back of her head. "Better give it to him straight."

She swung around. "Shut your big mouth!"

"I would heed your brother's advice," Kepesake told her.

Linda eyed him warily and more color flooded into her face, making it look like a brick-red moon. "No decency," she muttered. "All that's past pulled out and stared at." She raised several of her chins and tried to look haughty. "For a short time after Roger and I came here, I was . . . I suppose you'd say I was Mr. Penndragon's mistress."

"When given a choice, you elected to remain on as a servant?"

"I jumped at the chance. He didn't love me anymore . . . I don't think he ever really did, but I adored him. I'd have stayed on if I'd had to be a scullery maid."

Ice-cold eyes sought her brother. "And you approved of this?"

Evans shrugged a narrow shoulder. "Didn't approve or disapprove, sir."

"A callous attitude toward a sixteen-year-old sister."

"To understand, sir, you'd have to know our family. Had four sisters, just like our mum. A regular tartar was our mum. She wore the pants in our house and neither Dad nor me had a chance. Nothing I say ever sways Linda."

"What about your niece? Same go for her?"

Linda gasped but Evans stolidly said, "Told Linda not to let Dolly come here. Then she sends the girl into the tower to work. Told her not to do that either. Told her if anyone knows—knew—what Mr. Penndragon was like, *she* should."

The red moon lifted toward Kepesake. "I thought he was . . . past it—too old."

"May have been getting on," Evans observed, "but he was still a *man*."

"I should have listened to Roger, Chief Inspector. That man went right after Dolly the same as he had me. I found them rolling around on his bed. He was pawing and slobbering all over her and Dolly was enjoying it. I slapped her and gave him a piece of my mind. He apologized and since then he didn't have a chance to get near the little flirt. I'm sending her back to her mother!"

"Could you have been jealous of your niece, Miss Evans?"

"No!" She hesitated and then said brokenly, "Yes, I guess I was. It brought back so many memories. And Dolly looks exactly like I did at her age."

Forsythe noticed Helm straightening at his post. The young constable was staring incredulously at the house-keeper's fat body overflowing her chair. He shook his head.

Take a good look, Forsythe advised him silently, that's delicious Dolly in a few years.

The chief inspector was still toying with the jade. "You do know that under Mr. Penndragon's will both of you will be receiving sizable legacies."

Linda seemed to have lost all desire to talk and it was Roger Evans who answered. "The master told us, sir, said we'd be well looked after if anything happened to him. Very generous."

"Have you plans for the future? Will you stay on here?"

"I don't know whether Mr. Bunny will keep this house, sir, but I'm getting on and I've always wanted a place of my own . . . maybe in Brighton." His dour face was close to cheerful. "I've always liked fishing."

"And you, Miss Evans?"

"Don't know," she mumbled. "Can I . . . can we go?"

Kepesake dismissed them. Linda led the way, sagging rather than bouncing. Her brother lingered at the door long enough to turn and, surprisingly, lowered one eyelid in a roguish wink.

Sergeant Brummell grinned. "Chap enjoyed your cutting his sister down to size."

"That was a thorough job you did on her," Forsythe remarked.

Lifting his chin, Kepesake looked haughty without effort. "Long overdue. I've disliked her for years. She's far too familiar. Forgets her place."

Brummell winked at the barrister. "Never mind, Chief, doubt she'll even *think* of you as Adam from now on."

CHAPTER 12

A<small>DAM</small> K<small>EPESAKE</small> <small>STRETCHED AND THEN GOT TO HIS FEET.</small> Restlessly, he paced the length of the library, pausing to glance at Krimshaw's notebook, stopping to gaze from a window. All that could be heard was the crackle of wood on the hearth, the lashing rain against the panes, Helm moving at his post by the door. Turning back from the dismal view, Kepesake said, "You can take a break, lads. Walk around and stretch your legs."

Krimshaw got up with alacrity and Helm looked at the mantel clock. "Nearly one, sir. All right to look up some lunch?"

"By all means. Have some sent in to us."

As Kepesake leaned gracefully against the mantel, Forsythe decided that something about the man reminded him of Winslow Penndragon, not in his physical resemblance, but perhaps in his grooming and clothes—the well-cut suit, silk tie, a glimpse of matching silk above highly polished shoes, above all, an aura of arrogance.

The sergeant was watching Kepesake too and his eyes were fond. "Any ideas, Chief?"

"A number, and time to kick them around. Forsythe, do you have any thoughts?"

"Only the two I mentioned to Beau last night and one's been explained."

"The neatness of the bed?"

"Yes. Obviously it must have been straightened after the murder. But the murder weapon still puzzles me."

"I'm inclined to agree with Beau. The cherub was handy and the killer simply grabbed it."

"Perhaps. But still . . ."

Bending, Kepesake poked at the logs. A shower of sparks flew up. "Beau?"

"I've a fair idea now how the crime was committed. Mr. Penndragon was in bed, relaxing and looking over that material in the folder. It was some time after one A.M. Two people entered his room. Perhaps he was surprised but not alarmed. They walked over to the bed and one of them leaped on him and straddled his body, holding his shoulders down—"

"Why straddle? Surely that person could have circled the bed and grasped his shoulders?"

"Won't work, Chief. That's a wide bed. Awkward to try and stand on the far side and hold Mr. Penndragon down. Besides, for a man of your godfather's age, he was in good shape. A lot easier to pin him down by kneeling across his chest."

"That does make sense. Then?"

"The one wearing the Burberry and the mitts picked up the cherub and knocked the old gentleman out."

"Your reasoning?"

"The messiest job. Think of the amount of blood on that Burberry. The person holding him down could have leaned back and probably only the hands would have gotten spattered. Then the killer flailed at the head and face of the victim and when it was finished, they straightened up the bedclothes, put the cherub on his chest, went down to the main house, replaced the Burberry on a peg, and toddled quietly off to their rooms."

Kepesake nodded sagely and asked the barrister, "That agree with your reasoning?"

"Precisely."

"Mine too. Now, we need two people acting as partners. We have seven possibles. It could be Evans and his sister—"

Forsythe interrupted. "I don't get the impression they get along well enough to be partners at anything."

"Appearances can be deceiving. That could have been an act. Evans may well have resented his sister and young niece being used as . . . as conveniences. And there's Linda. That scene with Dolly could have well made her homicidal—the woman scorned, old boy. Then there're nice fat chunks of money coming as legacies. Worth considering?"

"It is, Chief."

Wandering back to the window, Kepesake gazed out. His voice was muffled. "I'm considering Aunt Grace."

"Don't think her son was her partner, Chief."

"Neither do I. There has never been a closeness between them. Anyway, both Aunt Grace and Bunny were at the tennis court. I was thinking of Jarvis."

"The gardener?" Forsythe asked.

"He's been here almost as long as Aunt Grace has. And Jarvis likes her. She potters around the grounds with him, chats with him. Took his side when Uncle Winslow found fault with his work. Look how Aunt Grace got the old fellow to talk after Uncle Winslow swore him to silence. Remember, Jarvis is also mentioned in the will."

Forsythe considered. An unlikely pair but possible. Kepesake turned back from the window. "Then there's Aunt Grace with another partner. I've been considering Miss Vandervoort. And her motive is clear—her mother's alcoholism and early death."

The barrister shook his head. "You've read what Miss Vandervoort told me about her mother's family. She didn't

154

blame her father for that or for leaving her to be raised by a stepfather."

"She could have been lying, old boy." Kepesake added indulgently, "You do tend to be rather gullible when it comes to fair maidens."

"You've forgotten something, Chief. Miss Vandervoort saved her father's life at the gardening shed."

"True, Beau, that had slipped my mind." Kepesake frowned. "Very well, on to the next likely pair—Leslie Hobbs and Cesar Guevarro. Opportunity and motive there."

"Pretty foolish move on Guevarro's part," Brummell said flatly. "Fixing those brakes, I mean."

"We'll pass on. I'm trying to work Jason Cooper in."

"Not going to be easy," Brummell grunted. "Can't picture him working with anyone. He's a loner. Seems to me he'd do his killing alone."

"Maybe not. I'm thinking of him and his half brother."

"Mr. Hobbs? I thought you just said Guevarro and—"

"Beau, I'm simply tossing ideas around. But think of it, two brothers, sharing a mutual hatred of a father. Hoping to gain more from Bunny than they could from that father. I've seen weaker motives for murder than that."

They all had. Again the silence was broken only by a gust of rain driven against the side of the house. Suddenly, the door was flung open. "Helm," Kepesake said, "with luncheon."

It wasn't Helm. Mis Sanderson carried the tray. Her face was pink and she darted a defiant look at the barrister. "I was in the kitchen when the constables came in. Linda isn't making lunch. She seemed distraught and went up to her room and the cook, of course, is still in bed. So I got something for Krimshaw and Helm and for us." She looked appealingly at Kepesake. "Mind if I lunch with you?"

"Not at all, Miss Sanderson. In fact, I'm delighted to see you." He gallantly took the tray from her and placed it on a table. "Keeping busy?"

"At what?" She made a face. "Spent most of the time lurking up in our rooms. When I did venture down it was sticky."

"People hostile?"

"People acting as though I'm the invisible woman. Looking through me. The only ones who talked to me were Grace and, oddly enough, the Sphinx." Kepesake looked his question and she smiled. "That's what Grace calls Jason Cooper."

"An apt name." He circled the desk to the swivel chair. "What do you have for us?"

"I remembered Beau likes beer." She put a bottle and glass down before the sergeant who gave her an appreciative smile. "Coffee for us, Adam. Milk for Robby."

"Sandy, I don't want milk."

"Don't be petulant. You've been living on whiskey, coffee, and painkillers."

"Dangerous diet," Kepesake agreed. "Be a good boy and drink your milk."

Forsythe glowered while Miss Sanderson lifted dishes onto the desk. "Pickles here, and a plate of sandwiches." She held the plate out to the policemen. "Two kinds— salmon paste this side, egg salad over here."

Kepesake helped himself to two salmon triangles and two of egg salad. Brummell pondered and then reached for the egg salad. Twirling the plate, Abigail set it down in front of the barrister. He transferred his glower to the sandwiches. "Robby, stop sulking and eat. Adam, any chance of me having a peek at the reports thus far? I'm not being nosy . . . or maybe I am, but I'm completely in the dark."

"Welcome to the club," Kepesake said wryly. "That brings our membership to four. Forsythe is still brooding about the murder weapon; Beau is concentrating on the scene of the crime; and I'm grabbing at one pair for killers and then another. By all means look over what we have. Maybe you'll notice something we've overlooked."

"That murky, eh? After lunch, I'll try my luck. Robby, you simply must eat and that's an order!"

Neither Brummell nor Kepesake bothered hiding their amusement. Miss Sanderson had spoken to Forsythe as though he were a small boy. With obvious reluctance he reached for a sandwich. He was lifting a triangle toward his mouth when he stopped, held it suspended, and frowned at it. Then he said slowly, "Sandy, do that again."

"Do what?"

"Hand around the plate."

"But—"

"Do it!"

She sighed, picked up the plate, and solemnly offered it first to the chief inspector, then to the sergeant. The men pantomimed taking sandwiches and then she turned, twirled the plate, and set it in front of Forsythe. "Salmon paste," he muttered and put down the sandwich untasted.

Brummell and Kepesake leaned forward, their eyes fastened on the barrister. Kepesake said, "Have you thought of—"

Forsythe held up his hand and the chief inspector broke off. No one moved or spoke and finally Forsythe lifted his head and regarded Kepesake. In that look, there was a trace of pity. "Adam, after what you've learned about your godfather . . . do you still feel the death penalty should be reinstated?"

"Nothing I've heard has changed my mind about that. He was brutally killed and no matter what his private life was, he didn't deserve that."

"You may change your mind."

"For God's sake, Forsythe, get on with it!"

"Part of this is conjecture, but some of it can be verified—"

"How does a salmon sandwich enter into it?"

"Hold on and I'll explain. The day after Sandy and I arrived, there was a special tea. Mrs. Krugger had baked a cake and—"

As he spoke, his listeners' expressions changed from eagerness to dismay and then to sick comprehension. All looked older and immeasurably saddened. Forsythe didn't speak quickly and his voice dragged; he hesitated frequently, but finally he finished. Kepesake bowed his head. "This sort of thing . . . it can't happen."

"I'm afraid it has," Forsythe muttered.

Brummell straightened his sagging shoulders. "One way to make sure." Without asking for Kepesake's permission, he pulled the telephone over and dialed. He spoke rapidly and then put a hand over the mouthpiece. "Mr. Forsythe, any idea about time?"

It was his secretary who said, "Late October or possibly early November of last year."

He relayed the information and rang off. "Now we wait."

They waited. Miss Sanderson cleared the desk, piling plates and cups on the tray. Adam Kepesake roamed around the room, lifting a log onto the grate, pulling back velvet curtains to peer out at the dreary day. The room darkened and he switched table lamps on. Helm stuck his head in the door and was told to get out. The sergeant sat stolidly, his eyes following the chief inspector, flicking toward the clock. It seemed a lifetime before the telephone rang. In time, it had been less than three hours.

Brummell took the call, jotted down a couple of notes, replaced the receiver. He said, "October the twenty-eighth. In London. Chief?"

Kepesake had halted by the window, his back toward the rest. He said softly, "Primitive feeling, vengeance. An eye for an eye, a tooth— Now I know vengeance *was* done and Winslow Penndragon got exactly what he had coming to him."

"Adam," Forsythe said sharply. "Don't swing too far the other way."

Kepesake spun around. "Tell me this. What would it have cost him? A few minutes of his precious time. But in his wonderful world, there was no time, no thought for anyone but himself." He walked back to the desk and sank heavily on the chair. "I take no pleasure in this."

"But it has to be done, Chief." Brummell touched the other man's shoulder. "Want the lads in now?"

"Yes."

As Brummell left to locate the constables, Miss Sanderson darted an imploring look at Forsythe. He started to push himself up. "Where are you going?" Kepesake asked.

"You no longer need us."

"I would like you to stay." He added, "Robert."

When Brummell returned with Krimshaw and Helm, the chief inspector said, "Helm, would you ask—"

A soft tap sounded on the door and Helm turned to open it. On the threshold stood Susan Vandervoort. No longer did she look like a ghost. Makeup discreetly brightened her cheeks and lips; rose-colored linen swirled around her slender figure. Girding her waist was a chain belt, silver this time. She glanced around the room and then fixed dove gray eyes on the chief inspector. "Sorry to intrude, but Sergeant Brummell said he would speak with you."

"About your father's condition." Kepesake rose. "Yes, he did mention it. Would you be seated, Miss Vandervoort."

She took the chair opposite him. "It would be a great kindness if you would let me go to him."

"You'll be leaving shortly. Helm, would you ask Mr. Cooper to step in."

She glanced over her shoulder. "What has Jason to do with my father?"

"Patience, Miss Vandervoort."

When Jason arrived and had accepted a chair drawn up beside his half sister's, Kepesake nodded to his sergeant. Stepping forward, Brummell cleared his throat, and said gruffly, "Susan Barbara Vandervoort and Jason Jacob Cooper, you are charged with the murder of Winslow Maxwell Penndragon on the . . ."

159

As his voice droned on Miss Sanderson made a sound deep in her throat. Forsythe's eyes flew to her and he whispered, "Get out of here, Sandy. Find Grace and stay with her." She practically ran to the door, brushed past Helm, and disappeared.

Jason didn't move a muscle while Brummell spoke, but Susan started up. "Are you mad?"

Kepesake told her, "If you wish your solicitor present—"

"I asked whether you were mad."

Without taking his eyes off the chief inspector, Jason said, "Let's hear him out."

"Thank you, Mr. Cooper. We've established that on October the twenty-eighth of last year a civil ceremony was conducted in London uniting in the bonds of holy matrimony Susan Vandervoort, resident of that city, and Jason Cooper, resident of Mousehole, Cornwall. I'll ask you once more. Do you wish to have your solicitor present?"

Jason shook his head. After a moment, Susan whispered, "No."

"Would you like to make a statement?"

Again Jason's dark head moved in a negative gesture, but Susan said wearily, "Why not? The only reason we've tried to conceal this is because of my father. I wanted time to be with him when he dies."

"Whether you make a statement or not, Miss Vandervoort, you'll be escorted to your father. That I promise."

"In that case, we'll give you a statement. Jason, could you . . ,"

He half turned toward her, sighed, and turned back to face Kepesake. "In a way, this will be a relief. Where will I start?"

"When you went to London last fall would be the best place."

"Very well. As you know, I went to London to make arrangements for a new shop. It was a totally new experience for me and for a time, I simply enjoyed the novelty of being on my own. Then I began to feel a bit guilty about my mother and, to salve my conscience, decided to buy her a gift. I went to the women's department of a large store and looked over their selection of bed jackets. I found one in her favorite color, but it was much too large. The clerk mentioned something about the buyer, left, and returned with a lovely blond girl—a Miss Susan Vandervoort. She assured me that she could order the jacket in Mother's size and I gave her the address for delivery and so on."

The young man had been speaking in his usual clipped way, but now his voice slowed. "I wasn't accustomed to talking to attractive girls. Mama disapproved of anything like that. But I looked across the counter at Susan, smiling at me with that soft blue jacket in her hands . . . something happened. When she started back to her office, I took my courage in both hands and followed. I didn't know what to say. I'm not glib and self-confident."

He looked sideways at Susan and she nodded. "He was certainly far from that. He stuttered and shuffled his feet and finally blurted out that he was a stranger in the city and asked whether I would have a drink or coffee with him. I suggested we go along to the cafeteria and we did. Afterward Jason told me it had been an instant attraction with him and it had with me too. It was like . . . like looking up and seeing something you've always hungered for and never found—the other half of a whole.

"We talked; we found we had the same taste in music, in books. Our backgrounds were not dissimilar. Jason's mother had kept him away from other young people and my mother's illness had done the same to me. While she was alive, I didn't dare take friends home. Her condition . . . it was too embarrassing. After her death, my father and I had to work so hard just to keep afloat. Father and I made a cosy little world for ourselves and I didn't feel the need for anyone else until he became ill."

"We were both so terribly lonely," Jason recalled. "So

eager for love. We spent every moment we could together and that wasn't enough, so . . . we married." The mask fell away from his fine features and under it was sickness and horror. "I had fallen in love with and married my own half sister."

"For a time you didn't realize that," Forsythe said.

"No," the girl said unsteadily. "For a time we didn't know. Jason and I decided to keep our marriage a secret because of his mother."

"She had so little time left," Jason said. "And Mama would have been heartbroken. She would have felt I had deserted her. I urged Susan to tell her father, but she wouldn't. She said there would be lots of time."

Taking out his jade holder, Kepesake stared down at it and then put it on the desk. "You were still registered in your hotel, Mr. Cooper."

"A place for mail and telephone calls only. Every afternoon, I'd wait for Susan to leave the store and we'd go to her flat. Time passed, a magical time, and then I was called back to Mousehole. As soon as I left Mama's room each evening, I'd go to a phone booth in the lobby of the hospital and ring up Susan. One night . . ."

"I had marvelous news for Jason," Susan said bitterly. "We wanted children, a number of them. We planned on a large family. I told him I was pregnant." The gray eyes fastened on Forsythe. "Did you know that?"

"Guessed. The cherub, the statue of a little girl, that remark you made about little Lucy that so upset Sandy."

"I was pregnant with my half brother's child. A child who could be . . . it might have been a monster." A shudder shook her slender frame and she buried her face in her hands.

Kepesake gazed at her bowed head and his hands clenched into fists. It was Sergeant Brummell who asked, "When did you discover your relationship?"

Susan didn't lift her head and it was Jason who said, "The day that *he* came to the hospital to visit my mother.

He'd seen Susan the day before. My mother was very ill and clinging to me and I hadn't been able to leave her to make my daily call to my wife . . . to Susan. After Mother introduced me to him, she asked me to leave them and so I went to the lobby and rang Susan up. I remember laughing when I told her about my long-lost father—"

"Who was *my* long-lost father." The girl's head jerked up, the flaxen hair spilled away from her face, makeup stood out starkly against her drained skin, making her look clownlike. "I can't tell you how I felt. I knew I *never* wanted to see Jason again, but I had to. After his mother's funeral, he came to my flat."

Jason reached out a hand toward her and she flinched away. "She was close to mad. The Christmas tree was still standing, but she'd taken off all the children's figures and smashed them."

"I first smashed the ones *he* had sent me for a bribe. You see, I'd aborted my baby." Her voice rose shrilly. "I'd murdered my own baby!"

"Susan had cut her foot on a shard of porcelain. It was covered with blood and she wouldn't . . . she wouldn't let me touch her to bandage it. I still loved her; I'll always love her." Jason looked from one man to another. "We *had* to do something."

It was Forsythe who said, "You accepted your father's invitation and came to Penndragon to kill him."

"No," Susan whispered. "We came to destroy something he loved as he'd destroyed us, destroyed our baby. Jason and I pretended to be strangers and we watched him closely. At first, we thought he loved his nephew—"

"You'd have killed Bunny?" Kepesake asked.

"If Winnie had loved him enough—yes. But we soon realized he loved nothing. He took us through his tower and we wondered whether he loved his paintings and jade and china. He didn't. He only collected; he had little feeling for beauty. In this entire world, there was only one thing he loved—himself."

163

Jason smiled, that wolfish grimace merely baring his teeth. "Then we hit on it. He told both of us about his grandfather's and father's long lives. He kept boasting he had thirty years left to enjoy his wonderful life. We took them away from him."

Brummell was as impassive as the younger man had been earlier. "Mr. Cooper, you loosened the brake connection on the Bentley."

"I did."

"Miss Vandervoort, you placed the marble statue over the door of the shed."

"Yes."

"Then why did you call to him and save his life?"

"While I was waiting for him to open that door, I realized it wasn't enough. The statue would fall and he would be dead. Never knowing why, never knowing he was losing his precious thirty years. He didn't deserve an easy death."

Kepesake stirred. "Had you made plans to kill him that night?"

Jason's lips pulled away from his teeth again. "We knew why Mr. Forsythe and Miss Sanderson were here, but we weren't going to let them stop us. We were watching for the first chance to finish him off. When Leslie asked for that sleeping capsule, it came. I lied about not having taken one. I did and it was powerful. As soon as Leslie was sound asleep, Susan and I went to the tower. She wore Grace's Burberry and those red mitts—"

"I'd already decided to use the cherub," Susan interrupted. "He showed it to me so proudly and it looked . . . it looked like a beautiful baby. It seemed fitting. When we got to his bedroom, he was in bed, reading some papers. He was surprised but not alarmed. He made a joke about the coat and mitts, asked whether I was in disguise. Jason leaped on the bed and held him down. Then we told him all about our marriage and about our baby. We told him he was going to die. We expected him to beg, to plead for mercy, perhaps weep."

"He didn't," Kepesake said in a muffled voice. "Winslow Penndragon was many things, but he was valiant."

"He was," Jason said. "He didn't even struggle. Just lay back, smiled, and told us to go ahead."

"I struck his head," the girl told them. "Jason jumped back and I struck him again and again." One fist pounded her other palm. "Again and again until his head was a bloody pulp. That face of his was just a mass of bone and blood."

Kepesake was watching the fist rising and falling. "*Don't*. Was it worth it?"

Her hands stilled. "I destroyed his face and do you know what I see in my mirror? That face! I'd like . . . I want to destroy my own face. I'll never be free of him. Never!"

Jason sagged in his chair. "It changed nothing. All our memories . . . our lives are useless to us. God! I wish they still executed murderers. Oblivion . . ."

The chief inspector looked from the man to the girl— Susan's fair beauty, her brother's dark good looks, their different coloring, the same bone structure. "I'm *glad* it no longer is in effect. You've been punished enough already, but, yes, you'll always live with it. Even society doesn't practice that sort of torment. Miss Vandervoort, as soon as your statement is signed, I'll take you to your father."

Forsythe could stand no more. He rose stiffly and hobbled from the room.

EPILOGUE

WHEN HE REACHED THE MORNING ROOM, HE FOUND IT cosy with lamplight, firelight, and heavy curtains drawn against the dark and the storm. Miss Sanderson huddled in an armchair on one side of the hearth and opposite her, perched on an armless chair, was Grace Penndragon. She was wearing a trim gray dress and steel needles flashed in her hands. Forsythe noticed the length of knitting suspended. The Argyle sock was nearly finished.

Without turning her head, his secretary said, "Are they . . . Have they left yet?"

"Not yet, but soon. Adam is taking the girl to the nursing home in London. I rang through for a rented car. Sandy, we're leaving. Would you go up and pack our cases?"

She got up and, as she opened the door, touched his arm. "Robby," she whispered and then she was gone.

"She's taking it hard," Grace said.

"Her emotions are still raw after that nightmare in Maddersley. Did she tell you about your niece and nephew?"

"She didn't have to. I already knew."

Forsythe sank down in the chair that Miss Sanderson had used. The cushions were still warm from her body. Putting her knitting aside, Grace poured brandy and handed the barrister a glass. "We can both use this, Mr. Forsythe."

"How long have you known?"

"From the evening that Susan arrived, I knew Jason and she weren't strangers."

"How?"

"Jason gave it away. When Evans brought Susan from the train, Winslow had all of us into the drawing room to meet his daughter. Jason and Susan went to elaborate lengths to show they had never met before. Winslow asked Jason to help him at the drink table and, while Winslow made up drinks to order, Jason poured soda in a glass, crossed the room, and handed it to Susan. She hadn't said what she wished and at that time none of us was aware she didn't touch alcohol. Winslow was excited, Leslie upset, Bunny fascinated by Susan. I was the only one who caught it. So I knew they were acting and waited to see what it was all about."

She paused and tugged on a ball of yellow wool. "They were good actors, but they did make another slip. I was hoping you wouldn't catch it."

"At the time I certainly didn't. Then today Sandy did something and I suddenly saw that silver cake plate piled with cherry cake and tarts. Sandy did this." He picked up a large ashtray. "She'd cut two kinds of sandwiches, salmon paste on this side, egg salad on the other. She served Adam and Beau and when she put the plate down in front of me, she turned it so the salmon sandwiches were facing me. Sandy knows I detest egg salad. Which is the point. When Susan put the cake plate down in front of Jason at tea that day, she did the same thing—turned it so the tarts were facing him. Yet, at that time, no one was supposed to know that he's allergic to cherries."

"And then you considered the information both of us had?"

"The questions that seemed to have no answers. Winslow told Sandy and me about his first meeting with his daughter. A happy, cheerful girl who appeared only amused to be told he was her father. The girl who arrived here later—depressed, ill, obviously hating him. Why the change?"

"I'd hoped you'd put it down to worry over her stepfather."

"I did . . . until today. But would worry account for her loathing for her real father? No, so something had happened, something traumatic. Something concerning her and Jason."

Grace sighed. "The same line of reasoning I took much earlier. Jason had been in London. Suppose they'd met, fallen in love, perhaps married . . ."

"Did you realize a baby had been conceived and been aborted?"

"Suspected it. Susan seemed so ill and that statue . . . such a charming figure of a small girl. The cherub was the picture of a fat little baby. Then the remark that so upset Miss Sanderson. Poor Susan, trying to persuade herself she'd made the right move in aborting her baby."

"Which you immediately tried to cover by diverting attention to yourself."

"Chiming in on the terrible state of the world? Yes, Mr. Forsythe, I dragged every red herring I could think of across your path, but I couldn't divert you."

He looked grimly at her. "You knew and you let them kill Winslow."

"Yes. You see Winslow had claimed three more victims. Susan and Jason and their unborn child. If he'd lived, there would have been more—Bunny for one, also Hobbs. Winslow would happily have ruined his own son. Not now. I know Bunny will save his cousin's restaurant. Do you understand? Winslow *had* to die."

"Under no circumstances can I condone murder."

"I can. Jason and his sister had nothing left to lose. Winslow had already taken any chance of a decent life away from them."

Setting down his glass, he said firmly, "And I can't sit in judgment."

"I can." She began to cast off stitches. When she'd finished, she held up the sock. "If you want it, it's yours."

He took it. "Yes, I want it. I've earned it." Her eyes fell and he asked, "Have you made any plans? Will you stay on here?"

"If Bunny does and if he wants me. If he doesn't, I'll take a flat or cottage somewhere."

"He'll want you."

She gave him a ghost of her wicked grin. "Happy ending, eh? Mother and son falling into each other's arms, vowing lifelong devotion? Mr. Forsythe, there are no happy endings. But perhaps something can be saved from this tragedy. Perhaps my son and I can achieve a relationship of sorts." She rose. "I must go to Bunny. Tell him—"

"Be kind."

"I will. He loves the girl." Forsythe struggled up and towered over her diminutive figure. She smiled up at him and this time the smile was gentle. "For Bunny, I pray for a happy ending. Another girl he can love."

The door opened and Miss Sanderson stepped in. She was wearing a raincoat and Forsythe's topcoat was draped over an arm. "Time, Robby. The car's arrived and the driver's taking out the bags." Handing the coat to the barrister, she bent to kiss the older woman's cheek. *"Vaya con Dios,"* Miss Sanderson whispered.

A smile of surpassing sweetness touched the lips of the old woman. "My friends, may you also go with God," Grace Penndragon said.

About the Author

Also the author of A DEATH FOR ADONIS, A
DEATH FOR A DARLING, A DEATH FOR A
DANCER, and A DEATH FOR A DOCTOR, E. X.
Giroux lives in Surrey, British Columbia.